Conner and Jackson: The Boyd Brothers

By Matthew Reade

Copyright © 2007 by Matthew Reade
All rights reserved. Published by Matthew Reade
Cover art by DixiePress

First Edition
Printed in the United States

ISBN: 978-0-6152-2201-1

This book is dedicated to Conner Boyd's inspiration, Connor Gutman. I also dedicate this book to the sixth grade class and my sixth grade teacher, for their generous support of my writing

Table of Contents

Chapter 1: War's Call – 8
Chapter 2: The Ride to Hell – 10
Chapter 3: The German Stronghold – 14
Chapter 4: The Strange Message – 18
Chapter 5: Jailbreakers – 22
Chapter 6: Stowaway Cargo – 26
Chapter 7: Lucky Break – 30
Chapter 8: A Valiant Proposition – 32
Chapter 9: Operation Underground – 36
Chapter 10: Making the Leap – 42
Chapter 11: Under Blinds – 46
Chapter 12: Hazardous Cargo – 52
Chapter 13: Uxwwhujdoh – 58
Chapter 14: High Fever – 62
Chapter 15: Conflict at Home – 66
Chapter 16: Rendezvous Point – 72
Chapter 17: Midnight Flight – 76
Chapter 18: Arrival – 82
Chapter 19: Target in Sight – 86
Chapter 20: Operation Windbreaker – 92
Chapter 21: Ready for Launch – 96
Chapter 22: Infiltration – 100
Chapter 23: Countdown – 106
Chapter 24: Press Release – 110

About the Author – 112

Prologue

On a cold December night in 1921, a set of twin boys was born in a small cottage in Richmond, Virginia. Their names were Conner and Jackson Boyd.

Their mother was dead. She had died in childbirth. Their father had left them, and would never come back.

The door of the cottage opened and a young man came in. His face was pale as he walked toward the babies.

"What?" he muttered softly. He picked up the children, left the house, and trudged through the snow into the cold, starry night.

Chapter 1
War's Call

"Boys, get up!" a voice yelled.

Conner sighed and got up from his warm pillows.

"Okay, just give me a second!" he called as he pulled on a pair of pants. Grabbing a shirt, he whipped Jackson and walked out of the room.

Jackson jumped up out of bed, fully dressed, and tackled Conner in the hallway outside the bedroom. He laughed.

"That's cheap!" yelled Conner, who was totally restrained by him.

"Okay." Jackson let go of him and ran off, still laughing hard.

Conner got up slowly and walked down the hallway after him. "Always does that," he muttered.

Conner strode into the kitchen and found his breakfast lying on a table. He picked his plate up and walked out the door of his home to follow his brother.

The twins were now twenty-one years old, and had begun to serve in the Army only three months before.

"Jack," said Conner through a mouthful of egg. "This is awesome. Really gives you some energy."

Jackson showed off his now empty plate. "I'm already done."

"Great," said Conner sarcastically as he placed his now finished plate on a small desk outside. "Hand over yours."

Jackson shrugged. "Why do we need to do this anyway? Mark doesn't need to give us breakfast. We could eat in the mess hall at the training center." He handed Conner his plate, which was placed on top of his own.

Conner grimaced. "He doesn't want us to eat that nasty, just purely nasty food there! Why call it food?" he said disgustedly.

Jackson laughed as he broke into a jog. "I would agree, but..."

"Yes, it's filled with important things," interrupted Conner. "I don't really care. Mark's food is better anyway with more nutrients." He increased his speed to match Jackson.

"What's your proof, science boy?" asked Jackson.

"Hey!" exclaimed Conner.

Jackson pointed ahead. "There's the headquarters," he said. "That's where we need to be. They said it was important. I doubt it's anything."

Twenty minutes later, Jackson, Conner, and several other young men were seated around an ebony table. A man walked into the room and sat down at the head of the table. Everyone quieted.

"Hello comrades, I am General Edison Starr. I have some information to share with you."

Jackson shifted uncomfortably.

"Several days ago, our forces were attacked at Pearl Harbor. We have only just officially declared war on the Japanese, the Germans, and the rest of the Axis powers," announced General Starr gravely. "The United States is selecting recruits to travel to the coastline and help free the coastal regions from Germany's iron grip. You will have the option of going. Please raise your hands if you want to stay."

No hands went up.

"All right," said Starr. "I am finished here then. Prepare your packs and weapons. We are leaving tomorrow."

The men all stood up from the table and began to leave.

Conner grimaced. "Sounds like we're all going to die," he said.

Chapter 2
The Ride to Hell

The next day, Conner and Jackson got up early and left the house silently. They walked down the icy streets toward the airfield near them, where they would secretly board a Curtiss C-46 Commando transport. If the flight went as planned, they would suit up and parachute down into an Allied base.

Conner hid his gun as the airfield appeared. He didn't want to attract any attention.

Jackson ran ahead and crouched behind a rock. "I see our transport," he announced. "Let's go."

They ran toward the rest of the men in their group.

"We were waiting for you!" exclaimed one of the recruits.

The pilot waved toward the men. "Get in, lads. This is going to be a tough ride."

Conner climbed up into the transport and sat down in one of the back seats. Jackson sat next to him before a tidal wave of men cascaded into the plane, pushing and jostling to find a seat.

The plane shuddered and took off, vibrating so fast that the passengers bounced up and down in their seats. Then finally, the plane steadied as it leveled out.

After many hours, Jackson fell asleep and began to snore peacefully. Conner also succumbed to the overcoming feeling of tiredness.

BOOM! The two men woke up, scared.

BOOM! Something hit the transport's wing, making it buckle and dive.

The pilot screamed. "Jump, lads, you have no choice!"

Conner, Jackson, and the rest of the men dove out of the plane with their parachutes. They landed on a field and tumbled to the ground.

A recruit near Conner screamed, and all hell broke loose.

Machine gun fire from an entrenchment ahead zipped into the tall grass. Conner felt something prick his ear and Jackson narrowly avoided getting shot in the head.

The aim of the machine guns would get better. In desperation, Conner clipped a grenade from his belt and threw it ahead. Then, he just got up and ran.

The smoke from the grenade made the machine gunners disoriented. They began to fire haphazardly into the smoke, trying to hit Conner. But this was to no avail, for he had already jumped over the first gun and tackled the gunners. Surprised, the men backed off, only to meet Jackson, who shot them in the chest.

Conner gave Jackson a thumbs-up, and they continued along the trench, taking out any Germans that they could see along the way.

* * * * *

One hundred miles away in a small town called Ruttergale, a German man adorned with medals paced around a small room, interrogating a British soldier.

"Where are the plans?" yelled the German commandingly.

The soldier was silent.

"If you don't tell me, I'll kill you," the German said quietly.

"Does it matter? Many others will die," the soldier remarked. "But you won't get the plans."

The interrogator grabbed him and threw him into a wall. "Don't test me!" he yelled hotly. "Guards!"

Three German soldiers opened the door and came in. "Yes sir?"

"Take him away!"

The British soldier was roughly lugged out of the room and the door shut.

The man rubbed his temple. This was going to be harder than he had thought.

* * * * *

Night overcame the trench, and the twin brothers were tired. They settled down in a small depression in the trench wall to get some needed rest.

Chapter 3
The German Stronghold

Conner woke up early in the morning to a sore back and no rations. He felt awfully hungry, but he could do nothing about it. He had no food with him, nor could he steal it from a German soldier.

Conner tapped Jackson, who immediately opened his eyes and stood up.

"Hey, Conner," he said alertly.

"Let's go," snapped Conner.

"Okay, okay, I'm going!" exclaimed Jackson. "Honestly…"

Conner put his hand over Jackson's mouth. "Shut up! Germans!" he whispered harshly as he crouched down.

Conner heard footsteps, which stopped quite near him. He was nervous and cocked his gun.

A bullet zipped through the barrel of his gun, rendering it useless. Gripping the gun, Conner rolled out of his hiding place and threw it at the tall German officer standing there.

Clunk! Conner's aim was perfect, and the rifle struck the man on the head. He crumpled pitifully to the ground, dead.

Conner removed the dead man's uniform and donned it, as well as taking his weapon, which was a modified Colt .45 American pistol. He examined the weapon and shoved it into his holster. It was better than nothing.

"Jackson," he called.

Jackson nodded.

"Watch my back," Conner said. "If you find a German soldier, knock him out and put on his uniform and take any passkeys you find. And stop slouching!"

Conner hauled him upright and walked off along the trench.

   * * * * *

The British soldier was roughly pushed into a truck and handcuffed. Two of the German soldiers hauled him upright and bundled him in a sack in the back. The other one started the truck and drove twelve blocks to the Ruttergale train station.

The soldier was removed from the sack and was escorted to a train. The German escorts gestured toward the heavily-armored vehicle and began to walk toward it with their prisoner.

"See that?" asked one of the soldiers. "That's your new home."

It was a monster. It was armed with fifteen cannons and sixty machine guns. The armor couldn't be punctured by a platoon of tanks. The prisoner couldn't even move from despair.

A ramp extended from an open door on the train, and the Germans shoved the man roughly through the door and shut it with a clang.

The prisoner sadly climbed into the small bed in the sealed compartment, trying to contain his fear as the train began to move.

*   *   *   *   *

Conner meandered along the trench, listening for signs of Germans. Finally, he spotted a score of German soldiers, talking quietly. However, his attention was focused on two soldiers standing next to a small tunnel in the wall.

Nervous, Conner approached the two men. "Permission to enter, sir?" Conner asked in a heavy German accent.

One of the soldiers raised an eyebrow. "Where is your passkey?"

Conner withdrew the pass from his pocket and showed the man.

"Go ahead!" The soldier opened a small grille on the entrance and gestured toward it.

Conner crouched down and crawled into the tunnel. Suddenly, it turned into a chute that descended down at a forty-five degree angle. After several seconds, Conner shot out of the chute and slammed into a metal railing. He slowly got up and looked around.

It was a huge underground building, filled with German soldiers and machinery. Men swung axes at a charcoal colored rock on some of the walls.

Conner wiped his forehead. He had to contact his allies.

But how?

Chapter 4
The Strange Message

It had been nearly a full day since the train had left Ruttergale, and the British soldier's door finally opened. His interrogator stalked in, followed by two guards.

The prisoner was tired but angry. "What are you doing here?" he asked, growling a bit.

The interrogator smiled. "My name is Commander Steil, if I haven't told you. I am here to ask the same question that I have asked you during your whole captivity. Where are the plans?" He held out a plate piled high with steaming beef, salad and mashed potatoes. "If you tell me," he coaxed. "You will get this much food four times a day. It will be just as good also." He scooped up a piece of beef and popped it into his mouth, chewing noisily. "So tender and delicious!"

The prisoner remained silent, though his face began to depict hunger.

"No?" asked Commander Steil persuasively. "Why not? Just a small bit of information and you will…"

"No!" yelled the prisoner. He collapsed onto his bed and pulled the covers over his face.

The guards smiled and laughed.

"Oh well," said Steil. "I can eat it!"

He left the room with his guards and slammed his door, laughing hard.

The prisoner peeked out from his covers. They were gone. He closed his eyes and fell into an uneasy sleep.

* * * * *

Conner walked down the metal stairs, heading toward one of the guards.

"Halt!" said the guard with a heavy German accent.

"Where is the communications room?" asked Conner.

The guard pointed toward a door. "Enter that door and you will be in the hallway. Then…"

The man narrowed his eyebrows. "Why don't you know where the communications room is?"

Conner moved his hand casually behind his own back.

"I know, I just wanted to check with you, but…" He swiftly drew his pistol, hitting the guard in the skull. The man crumpled.

"American! American!" yelled someone, and guards swarmed toward him.

Conner loaded the Colt and fired several times into the group of guards, and the front-runners fell to the ground, making their comrades trip over them. Conner winked and sprinted toward the door.

He gripped the doorknob and flung it open, ignoring the bullets whizzing over his head. Finally, after what seemed an hour, Conner slammed the door and locked it. Looking down the hallway, he saw a big table. He ran towards it, gripped the edge, and began to lug the table towards the shaking door. He moved the table next to the door. A perfect barricade.

Conner began to run down the hallway, trying to find the room. Suddenly, a German jumped from behind a cabinet and tackled him aggressively. Conner took something from his belt and thrust it upward.

The German slid to the floor, dead. Conner took the sword from the man's chest.

"Mark told me that this was on the bedside table when I was born," he muttered softly. "He said it belonged to my great, great, great grandfather."

He slipped the sword back into his belt and found the door. He opened it to find a radio. He sat down at a chair, thinking of a transmission to send.

* * * * *

General Edison Starr was having a difficult time. The recruits he had sent out were all dead, and the rescue groups sent to supposedly save any survivors were killed as well.

He sat pensively, watching a young boy at a radio. The boy was smiling, listening to the news.

Starr smiled. This was a nice respite from ordering people around.

Suddenly, the boy's smile faded, and static overcame the radio. The boy hid behind a desk as a soldier walked into the room and leaned toward the radio.

"General Starr, sir," said the man. "Please come here."

Starr got up slowly and walked toward the radio as the soldier hit a few buttons. "Listen to this," he said.

"This…Conner Boyd…I…infiltrated a…base in…"

Starr straightened in a heartbeat. "Ask him to repeat it," he said.

"Repeat name of place, sir," said the soldier into the mouthpiece.

"Somewhere off…coast…Fragul…Jackson…brother alive…"

General Starr looked delighted.

"Trench…filled…Germans," the voice said.

"Bombers on the way, sir," said the soldier.

Starr bolted upright. "He's still in there, though," he said.

The soldier smirked. "What the matter?" He pressed the call button.

*   *   *   *   *

Conner left the room at a run. He had to find a way out of the facility. He rounded a corner and ran into another man.

"Ouch!" exclaimed Conner.

The man grimaced and removed his German uniform. "Hey Conner," said Jackson. "It's me!"

Conner gave him a high-five. "We need to get out. This whole place is going to be bombed in a few minutes."

Jackson smiled despite the immense problem at hand. "We could use one of the planes in the hanger. I passed through there trying to find you."

"Let's go!" cried Conner.

Chapter 5
Jailbreakers

The prisoner woke up abruptly, sweating heavily. His dreams had been tainted by screams and cries of his comrades dying.

He wiped a hand across his forehead and stood up. He hated dreams. They always came at the wrong moment at the wrong time.

The British man crouched on the floor and sat against his bed. Something hit his leg. He stood up and backed away from the bed and slowly bent down.

It was a pistol, complete with several ammo packs. The prisoner smiled. There must have been a really smart prisoner in here, he thought as he stuffed it into his pocket.

He smiled wider as he pushed the bed across the room to the door. A barricade to stop the interrogator from getting in would help him if he was to kill the man. One more thing…

The prisoner reached into the seam of his pants and pulled out a pin. "This will work on the door," he said to himself as he slipped it into the keyhole and began to twist it furiously.

* * * * *

The young guard was sitting on the ground with a plate heaped with food when the British prisoner burst through the door that he was guarding. Before he could touch his weapon, he had been disarmed and thrown unceremoniously into the prisoner's room. His food was gone in a few seconds.

The German gazed up at the Brit. "What do you want from me?" he asked.

The prisoner smiled at him. "Give me all of your stuff and your uniform."

The man did as he requested.

"Now," said the Brit. "Stay here."

* * * * *

Conner and Jackson dove into the hanger behind a pile of barrels for cover as a hail of gunfire assaulted them. "What is up with these people?" asked Jackson, shooting a German pilot in the head three times, finally knocking him to the ground. "They won't die!"

Conner bared his teeth as he pummeled two officers with a hail of bullets. "Where did you get that rifle, bro?" he called over the shots.

His brother smiled. "I stole it from an officer."

Conner smiled as he shot another five, killing them. "Good job!"

The brothers eliminated the Germans quickly and moved on.

"There is the plane," said Jackson. "It's going to move the officers to a safer place."

Conner threw his brother behind a crate as the pilots in this area noticed them and began to fire. He jumped after his brother and fired a shot into the first one's leg. The man collapsed in pain.

That got the whole hanger angry. Every single pilot ran toward them in a tight group, threatening to overrun their protection.

Jackson threw a grenade desperately into the crowd and blasted the center away. Without three-quarters of its men, the group halted and was cut down easily.

Conner got up and ran toward the ship. "Come on, Jackson!"

Jackson joined him. Together, they sprinted toward the starting transport. The door was closing.

"Dive for it!" cried Conner.

The plane took off and the door sealed, leaving the brothers safe inside.

* * * * *

The prisoner walked through the train, moving toward the front. The Germans overlooked his disguise, muttering occasional hellos. Finally, he reached the control room. The train conductor was busy with the controls until a pistol shot brought him down.

The prisoner sat in his seat and pressed the red button in the center of the control set.

The train veered off the track and smashed into a tree, stopping suddenly. The collision created a chain reaction which ripped most of the train away. Everyone inside the back areas was killed. Finally, the front fell back onto the back, killing everyone else left inside.

The prisoner was already gone. He had escaped through a window a second before the crash.

But one other was left.

Commander Steil.

Chapter 6
Stowaway Cargo

The brothers huddled together under a table adjacent to the main entrance. Germans were everywhere.

Conner pointed his gun at an officer, but Jackson laid a hand on top of the pistol.

"Don't do it!" he whispered. "We'll get killed if you shoot him."

Conner ashamedly put it away. "We need to kill them somehow!"

Jackson smiled. "I'll deal with them," he said.

He skittered a grenade across the floor toward the large group of Germans. The grenade exploded before any of them noticed, and their bodies flew everywhere.

Conner and Jackson kicked away the table and stood up. They searched the place.

It was a cargo hold. There were many boxes on the floor, and crates were stacked up high. What got their attention most was the five barrels in the middle of the room.

The brothers exchanged glances and opened two of the barrels. They hopped inside and sealed them again.

* * * * *

"It's a beautiful night," said the prisoner. "The stars are all out. This is what I love about Europe."

He had been walking since the train crash, which occurred nearly twelve hours ago. He was tired and hungry, and he had no idea of where he was, only that he was somewhere in German territory.

"Yeah," he said to himself. "If only I could have some…"

He heard a buzzing noise. "What is that?"

It got louder.

"Planes," he swore. It was treeless. His only hope was to stay still.

Machine gun fire thudded into the ground next to him. He immediately dove to the ground and froze.

A searchlight came on, but it never passed over him. The plane moved on.

The prisoner breathed a sigh of relief. Slowly, he slipped away into a deep sleep.

* * * * *

General Starr paced around the radio room. He had heard no news from the attack. Finally, an exhilarated voice came unto the radio.

"Sir, the place is in ruins. Mission accomplished!"

Starr's brow was sweaty. "Any survivors?"

"No sir."

The general slumped into his chair and rubbed his eyes. "Where are you?" he asked.

The pilot's voice sounded again over the speakers. "We can see the ocean, sir."

General Starr studied the map on the wall. He traced his finger over Fragul. Where would those boys go? Finally, his hand settled upon Aurich. "Of course," he muttered.

"Soldier, get your crew refueled as soon as possible," he said loudly. "I want you back into the skies by eleven tomorrow night."

"Thank you, sir," said the pilot. "Glad to help."

The connection went dead and Starr stood up. He motioned toward the soldier standing at his door. "Fetch me the best assassins in this whole camp. I want to find those kids and get them safely home!"

* * * * *

A voice could be heard from outside the barrels. "We have the barrels, sir. They have all the space that you will need."

Someone stepped into the cargo hold as Conner and Jackson huddled into balls. "All right. Will any of them be heavy?"

"Yes."

The footsteps moved toward Conner's barrel and stopped. The person forced the barrel onto its side and rolled it away. Jackson's barrel was close behind.

The twins could feel hands gripping their barrels and pushing them into a steamy room.

"We'll leave this wine to ferment in here for a while," someone said.

"All right," said another voice, heavily anointed with a handsome Portuguese accent. "We'll leave them here."

The voices left, as did their owners.

The barrel lids popped open and the twins emerged, drenched with sweat and stiffened from the long wait.

"Oh man," breathed Conner as his leg crackled from standing. "That feels so good."

Jackson removed a small pistol from his belt and loaded it silently. "Let's find out where we are."

The brothers left the steamy room and walked down a hallway. They reached a turn and took it, entering a small room. A small man was standing in the middle of the room, his back to them. He was sipping a cup of coffee. Conner stealthily drew his gun from his belt and aimed it at the man. He motioned toward Jackson, who edged into the room and grabbed the man by the scruff of his neck.

"Freeze!" called Conner. "Or you die!"

The man dropped his coffee cup on the floor and held his hands in front of his face. "Don't shoot me! I've done no harm!"

Conner lowered the gun. "Where are we?" he asked harshly.

"Aurich!" chattered the man. "This is one of our military cargo centers. I know no more!"

Jackson threw him against the wall disdainfully. "Pathetic," he muttered.

Conner shoved the pistol into his belt. "Say nothing to anyone. Is there a way out of here?"

"There is a train leaving here in thirty minutes. It is headed to Rhaude."

"That's better than nothing," Jackson said. "That's not very far. We'll get there unnoticed."

"Thank you," said Conner.

The twins left the room and went into a corridor. They turned through a door and found themselves in the train station. German soldiers packed the trains and the space between the platforms.

The two glanced at the one armored train, standing regally at the center of the station. Only a few Germans were on top of the vehicle near the huge cannons. They smiled at each other and walked toward it.

Chapter 7
Lucky Break

The prisoner slowly woke from his deep sleep. Rubbing his eyes, he sat up and scanned the bright horizon. Nothing but hills lay ahead of him. He sighed and stood up. "Where am I?" he asked himself. On instinct, he turned his head.

"I think this is north," he muttered. He began to walk in the direction he had indicated.

* * * * *

Conner climbed a service ladder next the armored train and emerged on the top. He stealthily made his way toward the guns at the back of the train. There were three guards. One was sipping coffee and the other two were talking to each other. Conner smiled and headed toward them. He softly removed his gun from its holster as well. He pointed it toward the men, and with three flicks of the trigger, they all were lying on the ground, dead.

"Intruders!" cried a voice in the room, and all hell broke loose.

Machine guns chattered as Conner dove towards the large guns. Out of the corner of his eye, a German sniper steadied his weapon on a metal block and looked through the sight. Just before his hand could pull the trigger, a booming sound from the cannon at the front of the train sent a cannon shot into the man, blasting him into a wall. Conner looked toward the guns, nodded at a beaming Jackson, and fired a few cannon shots into the ceiling.

The ceiling began to crumble and the train began to move. Conner gripped a small handle on the floor and pulled hard to reveal another ladder that led into the train. With desperation on his face, he flung himself in and pulled the cover back down a second before the whole ceiling came down behind the train, leaving it to finish its journey.

* * * * *

Jackson fell from the ladder and crashed to the floor of the train. As he began to get up, a hand gripped the back of his shirt.

"Who are you?" said a slick voice.

"Why should I tell you?"

The hand dragged him upright. "Because you will die if you don't, is that good enough?"

Jackson smiled despite the threat. "No."

He was turned over. "Take him away!" said the voice before something hit his head, making everything black.

Chapter 8
A Valiant Proposition

Conner fell hard onto the floor. Painfully, he got up and picked up his pistol. He was about to load it, but froze when he heard muffled voices, speaking in German. He moved to the corner and was silent. The German men were getting closer.

With an aggressive twist, Conner turned into the hallway and pointed his pistol at the two men standing in the hallway. "Stop!" he called.

The men stopped. One held a mug of coffee and a croissant and the other held a rifle. "What are you doing? I thought you were a prisoner," said one in spotty English.

"Drop the rifle! I want it," demanded Conner.

The rifle fell to the floor.

"Now, give me the food."

The food was handed over and quickly downed.

"Thank you. Stay here," said Conner gratefully.

The coffee man beckoned him forward and pulled a map from his pocket. He pushed it toward Conner, who took it.

"Thank you again," Conner said. He smiled and ran down the hallway.

* * * * *

The former prisoner had been walking for about thirty minutes when he finally entered a small forest. The floor was littered with pine needles and small perennial flowers.

Suddenly, he heard a clink. He turned around to see Commander Steil. He gasped.

"You!" cried the prisoner.

"Yes, me!" exclaimed Steil. "Strange that I see you again, isn't it?" He drew a pistol and pointed it at the man's head.

The Brit pulled out his gun as well, and Steil was stunned momentarily. "How did you get it?" he asked.

The former prisoner aimed his gun at Steil's head. "Game over, drop it."

The commander was forced to drop his weapon.

"Put your arms behind your head," called the Brit.

The unfortunate man obeyed.

"Give me any rope that you have."

The man again obliged and handed the former prisoner a long cord of rope.

"Walk to the tree."

He obeyed again.

"Stand still," finished the Brit as he tied the man to the tree. He tightened the knots, and then took Steil's supplies, which ranged from a shotgun to a small food pack. The former prisoner tried to eat as slowly as possible, but it was difficult, considering how hungry he was. He smiled, waved to the helpless, bound man and walked away into the forest.

* * * * *

Conner walked down the hallway in the train, his senses alert. There could be no mistakes if he was to make it to Rhaude and find his brother.

He looked at the map. It showed German encampments in the region. He turned the rough paper over and found several extra maps. One of the train, another was of Berlin, and the last depicted a small forested area near Rhaude.

He frowned. The train was guarded more heavily at the front, which was where his brother had fallen. He shoved the map back into his pocket and turned right. He was now facing a service door. Gritting his teeth, he pushed it open to reveal the landscape and the outside of the train. In a mighty burst of strength, Conner leapt onto the roof of the fast-moving train. He began to crawl forward, inching along the metal toward the manhole at the front of the train.

* * * * *

General Starr sat down at the head of the meeting table. "Men, we are on a mission," he said. "We are on a mission to find the two brothers, Conner and Jackson Boyd. We also are trying to find Sergeant James Farion from the British military. He is one of the few who knows about the plan. The plan to repulse the German war machine and push it into its own territory. He is believed to be in prison. However, Mr. Farion has certain knowledge about Germany that we don't know. We cannot, and will not, let him die because of our slow speed."

He took a breath. "You are the best assassins in the Allied Forces. You can find these men. However, exercise extreme caution. The Boyd brothers are very well-trained, and they have a family to prove it. One of their great grandparents was a commander in the Revolutionary War; another killed Napoleon Bonaparte and spared Britain from his purge. They won't be afraid to kill you if they don't know who you are."

General Starr stood up. "Leave, gentlemen; the pilots are waiting."

The assassins stood up from their seats and left the room.

Starr wiped a hand across his forehead and set off toward his office, thinking about what would happen to the Boyd brothers if they couldn't be found.

Chapter 9
Operation Underground

The prisoner trekked through the forest, growing tired and hungry. He hadn't seen a human for miles.

Suddenly, the man stumbled. He cried out and got up slowly. He turned to examine the small step in the ground that he had tripped on. He dusted it off a little bit and found that it led to another step. He changed his position to get a better view of the second step. It led down, so…

The ground trembled suddenly and broke. The prisoner fell into the hole.

He hit the bottom at about ten feet from the surface. The frantic prisoner tried to grip the walls to haul himself up, but there were no handholds. Angry, he kicked the side of the ditch. It broke apart easily, revealing a metal grille. The prisoner drew the shotgun and shot the lock, forcing it open. He then crawled into the grille, trying to find a way out.

* * * * *

It had been a while since Conner had started crawling toward the front of the train. Now, he was only a meter away from the manhole.

He grunted and pulled himself forward, finally getting a grip on the manhole cover. He pulled it open, levered himself in, and closed it.

He fell to the floor and quickly got up. Readying the rifle, he walked into the hallway ahead. His foot struck something strange and he looked down.

A small door was lodged into the ground. Levering it upward, Conner found a dark hallway dimly illuminated with candles. He glanced at the map. It looked like a prison of some sort. He grimaced, placed the map into his back pocket, and started down the dark hallway.

* * * * *

The Curtiss C-46 Commando transport flew high into the air. Assassin Vincent Stenvich's eyes swept the seemingly untouched landscape of Germany. "There is Aurich," called out Vincent. "Order the attack force to move in and secure the airstrip."

"Done, sir."

"Good. Land it, pilot."

The transport set down on the airstrip and Vincent immediately strapped on his gear; a sniper rifle, a small pistol, smoke grenades, a compass, and a small food pack.

"All right, let's move!" yelled the assassin. "Take control of the supply base."

The soldiers with him headed toward the large building ahead. A small group of Germans walked out of the building, their hands up.

"Disarm them," rapped Vincent.

The men were quickly separated from their weapons and tied up.

"Do you know where the Americans went?" Vincent yelled.

A small man nodded toward him sheepishly. "Yes. They asked me where the trains were going, and I told them about the one going to Rhaude…"

Vincent slapped the man and grabbed him by the scruff of his neck. "Are you absolutely certain of this?" he growled.

"Yes, sir! Yes!"

The assassin threw the man to the floor. "Take them to a secure base and prepare to plant charges in the central area. Are there any trains left?"

"No, sir," replied one of the Germans. "They were all destroyed. The ceiling collapsed."

Vincent began to walk back toward the transport. "I want General Starr on the radio now! Let's go!"

* * * * *

General Starr sipped some cocoa as he sat in the radio room. He was awaiting news from one of his assassins stationed in Aurich. Finally, the static left and the voice of Vincent Stenvich took its place. "Well, Starr, we have found something of importance."

The general listened with bated breath. "And…"

"We know for sure that the brothers are en route to Rhaude by train. We think that the train is an armored one, carrying prisoners, cargo; the whole thing. Nothing about Farion yet, though. Your orders, General?"

Starr's answer was immediate. "Track them down and bring them safely home; that's your order."

"Excellent, General." The line went dead.

* * * * *

Conner had ventured down the dim hallway for quite a while when he finally saw two hallways forking out from the main one. He made a quick move and darted into the right hallway. In front of him was a German guard. He was surprised, but he recovered quickly and smacked the barrel of his rifle to the side of Conner's head. Dazed, Conner stood up, only to take another hit from the gun. He slumped to the floor and looked up. In his now blurry vision, he could see the man preparing to shoot him. The man pulled the trigger…

Click! The gun didn't shoot. The guard looked down the barrel and realized that it was out of ammunition. He reached into his pocket for a magazine.

Conner slowly began to get up, but the German was moving fast. He removed the old magazine, snapped on the new one, and aimed toward the dazed American.

The sword hardly made any sound as it swiped the guard's head clean off. Conner wiped the blade on the man's shirt and replaced it in its sheath.

A distant scream shattered the silence. Conner immediately looked up.

"Jackson."

Conner ran toward the voice, confident that he would find his brother. Finally, he reached a small, dirty cell. In it were his brother and two Germans. The Germans were torturing him by poking sharp needles at his right arm, which was covered with spots of blood. Conner was enraged. He took the rifle from his belt and shot at the men.

They fell to the ground, dead. Jackson groaned with pain and fell to the floor. Conner shot the lock, forcing it to open and ran into the cell.

"Brother," he asked. "Are you all right?"

Jackson didn't respond.

"Jackson?"

"What, Conner? I'm tired," murmured Jackson.

Conner ripped strips from the dead soldiers' shirts and tied them to Jackson's arm. The injured man winced and sat up. "How are we going to get out of here?"

Conner shrugged. "We have to wait until it stops."

Suddenly, Jackson's face became sweaty. "Look behind you Conner!"

It was a tall, thin German holding a shotgun.

Conner rotated and shot the man between the eyes and turned around again.

Jackson looked toward the cell door. "Let's get out of here."

Conner smiled. "Let's go!"

* * * * *

The prisoner had been crawling through the small tunnel for quite a while when he reached a small door. He shot the lock and pushed it open.

Suddenly, the dirt beneath him broke and he began to roll down a huge chute. After a minute of rolling, he smacked into a dirt barrier, which broke apart easily. He then smacked into a hard rock floor.

He looked up to see that he was in a small storage room. He got up slowly and began to walk forward. Footsteps could be heard ahead of him. The prisoner hid behind a barrel and waited.

Chapter 10
Making the Leap

The prisoner held the shotgun tightly as the footsteps entered the room. He could barely hear their owners' voices.

"I take it that it isn't ready yet, Corporal."

"You are correct, sir."

The footsteps stopped.

"Where is the main piece, Corporal Hans?"

The feet of the Corporal became visible. Sweat coursed down the prisoner's face.

"They are stacked from here to that wall, sir."

"Move them to the vault, idiot." He walked off.

"Yes, sir."

The corporal took his radio and spoke into it loudly. "This is Corporal Hans. I want five men down here to help me with some fragile packages."

A voice answered quickly. "They're on the way."

The prisoner knew he had to do something before the men arrived. In a swift move, he jumped forward toward the unsuspecting man and pushed him forward into a box. The man tripped and fell, hitting the rock floor hard and slipping into unconsciousness. The deft prisoner then left the room, leaving no trace of being there.

* * * * *

Vincent Stenvich was glancing out the window of his transport when a flash of light from below took his attention. He smiled, knowing it was nothing more than a metal scrap. Suddenly, an explosion rocked the plane. The assassin swore and grabbed the seat in front of him for support.

"We are being attacked!" screamed the pilot. "Find the parachutes!"

"There aren't any," cried one of the soldiers.

"We're going to crash!" yelled the pilot. "Take cover!"

The plane curved downward and began to plummet toward the ground. The pilot hauled the control stick back, bringing the aircraft nearly level to the ground before it crash-landed into a meadow.

Vincent jumped out as the plane made its initial impact. He cried out when he hit the ground at nearly one hundred miles per hour. His arm blazed with pain and everything went black.

* * * * *

Conner and Jackson had made their way to the top of the train again. They found a small hollow on the train roof and lay there, nursing their wounds.

"How are we getting off this wreck?" asked Jackson.

Conner glanced at the map. "No idea."

Jackson winced. "Why don't we jump off the train?"

Conner smiled. "Great idea." We just need some rope."

"I have some from that dead German guy. I took his shotgun too."

"Great. And there is the hook I need," said Conner. He tied the rope to the large, rusty hook and grabbed the rope. "Hold on until we touch the ground!"

The two brothers pushed off the train and hung over the side. Their momentum sent them back toward the train and they smacked into the side. However, they held on. As they began to swing back out away from the train, Conner let go and pulled Jackson with him.

The move had been timed just right. They were close to the ground and their forward momentum was minimal. The two men hit the ground and lay there as the train passed them and moved on, going out of sight.

"Good timing," said Jackson weakly.

Conner smiled. "I know. Let's get out of here."

The brothers got up and walked away from the tracks, heading toward the distant trees ahead.

* * * * *

Vincent Stenvich ascended from his unconsciousness with a fiery pain in his left arm. Using his good hand, he sat up. He could only see bodies and the ruins of the plane, which had crashed into the forest.

The assassin knew that his arm was injured, but he had to complete his assignment. He was about to walk away from the scene but he heard a groan. Vincent looked toward the crash sight and saw a man struggling to get up from the ground.

"Help!" called the man.

Stenvich ran toward the man and helped him up. "What happened to you?" he asked, noticing blood on the man's shoulder.

"Nothing, it's just the pilot's blood," winced the man. "I just feel sore."

Vincent wasn't fazed. "Who are you?"

"I'm Private Travis McCarthy, one of your soldiers. I was at the back of the transport, so I went prone when the explosion happened." The soldier looked at Vincent's arm. "Aching arm, huh?"

The assassin nodded. "Yes."

Travis began to walk in an eastern direction. "All right, Vincent Stenvich, let's go!"

Chapter 11
Under Blinds

The prisoner walked through the hallways, trying to look inconspicuous. However, he knew that his clothes would soon give him away. Nodding to a man running past him, he turned right into a small room. In it was a German soldier, his back turned to the prisoner.

The prisoner gripped the shotgun and smacked it against the unsuspecting soldier's head. The man collapsed, dead, into the prisoner's arms. The man's uniform was quickly removed and put on. The keys that were in the German's pocket went into his. Then, the newly fitted Brit moved on down the halls, ready for what was yet to come.

* * * * *

Conner and Jackson had been walking for sometime when they smelled smoke in the air.

"What is that?" asked Jackson.

"I don't know," replied Conner as he ran forward. "Wait a minute."

He stopped and surveyed the scene. "There is a United States transport over here. It looks like it crashed!"

Jackson ran toward the smoking wreck. "Yeah, that's a Commando, all right. Let's check it out!"

The brothers ran to the blackened mess.

"Lord, help us," murmured Conner as he looked at the ground, which was strewn with bodies. "Did anyone live?"

Jackson looked inside the ruin. "I don't think so."

Conner took a shotgun from one of the corpses and gave it to Jackson. "Here's a gun for you. Let's keep going."

"Okay," replied Jackson, still looking vaguely at the ruin. "Let's go."

* * * * *

Vincent and Travis had traveled for some time when they reached a large pit in the ground.

"Hey, this is ten feet deep!" called Travis.

Vincent pointed toward the metal grille. "What is that?"

Travis looked at the small door as well. "Let me see," he said as he leapt into the hole. "It is unlocked. I'll check it out and tell you how it looks." He opened it and disappeared into the darkness.

"It's clear."

The assassin jumped into the pit as well and crawled through the metal grille.

After a while, the two men reached a small metal door. Once again, its lock was shot through. But there was a large hole in the dirt floor. The assassin motioned toward the hole and Travis nodded. Vincent jumped down the hole and disappeared. Travis waited for any news.

"Stenvich, are you okay?"

He heard nothing.

Travis fought his instincts to jump down after him. It could be dangerous. He grappled his way over the hole and pushed the door open. Then, the soldier continued to crawl down the passage.

*   *   *   *   *

Conner and Jackson had walked for some time when a gunshot sounded. They looked toward the noise, alert.

"What was that?" asked Jackson.

Conner was absolutely silent.

Suddenly, Conner whipped around and smacked his rifle into the German preparing to grab him. The man clutched his stomach and moaned. Before the twin could do anything else, a second soldier floored him with a mighty punch. He sailed through the air and smacked into the ground hard.

Jackson was frozen with shock, but recovered quickly. He shot the second soldier in the leg with his shotgun and punched him in the face. The German's leg collapsed and he fell to the ground, unconscious.

However, a third German was waiting behind a tree. He sprung out from behind it and hit Jackson hard with the stub of a sub-machine gun. Jackson fell to the ground, gasping for breath, and a final hit knocked him out.

Conner only had a few seconds before he was knocked out as well.

* * * * *

General Starr had just finished his morning coffee when a breathless soldier ran in.

"Sir, we lost contact with Stenvich!"

The man was immediately thrust aside by the fuming general.

"How?" cried Starr as he entered the radio room.

The man followed close behind him and sat at the radio. "I don't know, sir, but some of our commanders have predicted that their plane crashed over the forest near Rhaude."

General Starr sat back in his chair, stunned. "Could we get a squad over there?"

The soldier shook his head.

The general sighed. What now?

* * * * *

Vincent tumbled through the passage and smacked into the hard rock floor. His head ached horribly, but he had no time to complain, for there were five German soldiers staring at him.

"Attack!" yelled one of them, and they set down the boxes that they were carrying and drew their weapons. However, the assassin was much faster. He drew his pistol and fired five quick shots at the group. The Germans fell to the ground, dead.

Vincent was about to leave the scene when he spotted another German lying on the floor, hands up.

"Don't hurt me!" cried the man. "I'm Corporal Hans."

The assassin looked at him critically. "I really don't care. What's in those boxes?"

Corporal Hans was silent.

The assassin put his pistol to the side of the hapless German's head. "I'll kill you if you don't tell me," he growled.

Corporal Hans appeared to be struggling.

"I'll shoot…"

"I don't know!"

Vincent pulled the trigger and fired the weapon. Corporal Hans slumped to the ground, dead.

Grimacing, the assassin left the room and hid the pistol in his belt, knowing it would be useful later.

*   *   *   *   *

Conner woke up in a small, cramped prison cell. He was lying on a cold metal cot with no blankets. He got up from the cot and hunched over into a ball. It was freezing and damp and his only light was a small bulb overhead, hanging only by a few bare wires, which powered it as well. The wires went through a small hole in the ceiling, and then came out at the other side of the wall and were touching the outlet there.

The twin glanced at all of this and quickly realized that there was no way out. All of a sudden, he got an idea.

He removed his shirt and wrapped it around his hand. He grounded himself and gripped the wires. With a vicious jerk, he pulled the wires down towards him.

The wires flew from the outlet and disappeared inside the ceiling. The twin pulled again, and all of the wire fell to the floor. Smiling, he took one of the wires and shoved it into the keyhole. He turned it, and the lock clicked softly. Conner placed the wire on the floor, picked up the rest of the wire, and pushed the cell door open softly.

Suddenly, Conner heard someone walking towards the cell door. He shut the door and sat down in the cell, pretending to look depressed.

A German soldier passed the cell door.

Seizing his opportunity, the American poked the wires through the bars and touched the man with them.

The scream must have been heard for miles. The soldier fell to the ground; his body emitting black smoke.

Conner dropped the wires and opened the cell doors quietly. The coast was clear. He looked down the hallway and began to run.

* * * * *

The prisoner walked down a hallway, searching for the cell block. He knew that a prison break would distract the Germans long enough for him to get out of there.

He took a left. How would he get out anyway? The Brit turned right and saw a small gate guarded by a soldier. Summoning his courage, he walked to the man.

"I would like to enter the cell block, sir," he said.

The soldier turned toward the gate and consulted a small pamphlet on the wall. "Keys?"

He reached into his pocket and pulled out the keys. "Here, sir."

The German looked at the former prisoner and took the keys. "Excellent," the man said as he opened the gate. "Carry on."

The Brit made for the gate but quickly pulled out the shotgun and pointed it at the man's head. "Let all of the prisoners out. Now!" he cried.

The man was rather calm as he pressed the red button on the panel next to the gate. "There you are."

The former prisoner was taken aback by the man's calm. "How can you be so calm? I'm putting a gun to your head!"

The man removed his German uniform. "My name is Vincent Stenvich. I am an assassin for the United States military. My first primary objective is to find Conner and Jackson Boyd, American soldiers who were shot down during an attack on Fragul. My other objective is to find James Farion."

The prisoner looked up, his face dark. "I am James Farion."

Chapter 12
Hazardous Cargo

Conner had been walking down the hallway for several minutes when a rasping voice called his name.

"Conner, Conner!" whispered the voice.

The man looked to the cell on his left, and there was Jackson.

"Hey Conner," said Jackson. No strength was in his voice.

Conner smiled and gripped the cell bars. "Hey, Jack!"

Suddenly, the doors opened.

"Why did the doors just open?" asked Conner.

Jackson got up, a bit unsteady. "I don't know, but everyone is coming out!"

Every single prisoner was leaving their cells, looking down the hallways.

"Let's get out of here!" cried Conner.

They both began to run toward the exit of the cell block, hoping to escape the awful place.

"Wait!" called Jackson.

Conner turned around. "What?"

"The sword!"

The twin grimaced. "We'll find it. Let's go!"

* * * * *

A heavily medaled German man walked through the main control room. A man called from his computer. "Sir, we have a problem!"

The German's boots clicked across the floor. "What is the problem?"

The rather disturbed man motioned toward the screen. "Sir, it looks like all of the prison cells have opened."

The German grabbed the man's chair and twisted it around. "What do you think you should do, idiot? Get a squad there now. Exterminate them."

His face was sweaty with fear. "Yes, sir."

"Do it!"

The man began to radio the squads hastily.

The German adjusted the sword at the side of his belt and moved on, his boots clinking.

   *   *   *   *   *

Vincent Stenvich peeked around the corner. "Looks like the prison break is working," he said with satisfaction.

It was. The large mass of prisoners was visible down the hallway, moving as fast as it could. Leading the pack were two young men. They looked about eighteen years old to the seasoned assassin. As the group came closer, he could see that the men matched the descriptions of Conner and Jackson Boyd.

"Excellent, my mission is accomplished!" he exclaimed to James Farion. "There are the Boyd brothers. I'm certain!"

The men were coming close to rounding the corner.

"Prepare to grab them," whispered Farion.

As the brothers rounded the corner, they were quickly snatched up by the two men and pushed into a pile of boxes.

"Hey!" called Conner. "Don't touch me or my brother!"

James Farion's sleeve quickly covered the man's mouth as the prisoners moved past them and turned a corner.

"Who the hell are you two?" asked Jackson weakly.

The Brit removed his sleeves from Conner's mouth. "I am James Farion. I am a British soldier with special information about the operation that the Germans are planning. He is Vincent Stenvich, a United States assassin. He was sent to find you two and to get you to your home safely." Vincent nodded to the two and helped them out of the pile of boxes.

"We need to get the sword," said Conner.

Vincent scoffed. "Why do you need a sword? Is it going to save your life?"

"It has saved my life, and it is a family heirloom. I can't let that sword go into enemy hands. You should see that blade on that thing…"

Conner was interrupted by a distant burst of gunfire and a chorus of screams.

James glanced down the hallway quickly. "No. We need to get out of here."

A German soldier appeared up the hallway.

"We need to get back to the storage room," whispered Vincent. "I'll get him."

The assassin pulled out his sniper rifle, aimed it at the man, and fired. The man fell to the ground, dead.

"Follow us!" called James. He began to run ahead, with the assassin at his side and the twins close behind him.

*   *   *   *   *

The heavy boots clicked across the floor to the line of soldiers. "Are they dead?" asked the man.

"Yes, sir!" yelled one of the soldiers.

A man peeked down the hallway. "Sir, you have an important call."

The German didn't move. "Who wishes to waste my time?"

"It is Hitler, sir!"

The man went forward and took the radio he was holding. "Adolf," he asked, "what brings you to make this connection?"

"Wilhelm von Schreider! When is it going to be ready? I cannot wait forever!" called the dry voice of Adolf Hitler. "I need it now!"

"Relax, Hitler," soothed Wilhelm. "I have the boxes. The transport will be leaving in fifteen minutes."

A soldier ran into the hallway and stopped. "Sir, there are six dead bodies in the storage room!"

Wilhelm was in a fury. "Get our soldiers in there now to bring the boxes to the hanger!" he yelled. Then, in a much calmer voice, he said into the receiver, "Hitler, the boxes will be ready in five minutes. I promise."

The German listened as Adolf laughed. "They better be ready, or you know what will happen!"

The line went dead.

Wilhelm cursed and gave the radio back to the man. "Get back to work, idiot!" he yelled.

The man left as quickly as possible.

Wilhelm massaged his temples. "They will be ready," he murmured softly.

*   *   *   *   *

Vincent and James ushered the two brothers into the storage room. "Get into the hole!" they whispered.

The twins climbed into the chute and disappeared.

"Go, Farion," said Vincent softly. Quick footsteps could barely be heard down the hallway.

A man ran into the room. It was Travis.

"Quickly, Vincent!" he whispered. The footsteps were getting closer now.

James disappeared up the chute.

"Now!"

Vincent climbed up out of sight.

Travis rummaged through his belt, finally coming up with a smoke grenade. He took a deep breath and tossed it into the doorway.

As the first Germans came in, Travis climbed up the chute and disappeared. When he reached the top, he crawled as fast he could after Vincent. He pulled the pin on one of his grenades and flung it next to the chute opening.

The grenade exploded, creating a veritable landslide of rock and dirt to prevent the Germans from following them. Travis reached the surface with the others a second before the whole tunnel collapsed.

"Now, to get out of this ditch," said Vincent.

As if to answer him, a section of the ditch wall crumbled, forming a small ledge.

"I'll go first," announced James. He gripped the edge of the ledge and pulled himself up. He stabbed his rifle butt into the ground and with a heaving effort, pulled himself out.

Conner and Jackson went next, their muscular arms flexing handsomely as they climbed out. Vincent pulled himself up despite his aching arm. Travis was right after him.

"All right, where do we go now?" asked James.

Conner pulled the map out of his pocket. "The map here shows that there is a small German encampment equipped with a radio a few miles southeast of here. I'm pretty sure we could arrange a flight to pick us up."

Vincent shook his head. "The plane would have to fly over that killer forest. They must have a million anti-aircraft units in there!" he exclaimed.

Travis pulled a map from his back pocket. It showed Germany and the countries around it. "We could go to the Netherlands. It isn't far, and the Allies have a foothold back there."

"We could stay."

They all turned toward James.

"Why?" asked Conner.

"When I was in the supply room, I heard those Germans were talking about something, like the main piece wasn't ready," he stuttered. "They were obviously talking about something important. And I know what they might be doing."

"What, James?"

He took a deep breath.

"The Germans are planning an attack on the United States," said the former prisoner.

"What kind of attack?" asked Vincent.

James Farion's face was bleak. "A virus attack."

The first thing that Conner did was laugh. "You must be crazy!" he called, laughing hard.

Farion was still emotionless. "No, I'm not kidding. It is a modified version of a virus called Mandible. It looks like orange juice, but it will infect your organs and stop their work, of course, killing you."

Jackson slapped his brother. "Stop laughing, Conner. This is real!"

Conner stopped and glanced at James. "Are you sure?"

James nodded his head gravely. "Absolutely," he said. "Here's the worst part though. The virus is modified to not be noticed for several days, so when you find out that you have it, it is too late. It will have already spread to hundreds of people through your contact with them."

Jackson rubbed his arm unconsciously. "How is the virus controlled? And how does it get to the United States?"

The former prisoner shook his head. "I don't know the answer to those questions. What I have told you is the limit of my knowledge about this weapon," he said, looking into Jackson's eyes. He suddenly smote his forehead. "Oh yes, one possibly good thing. I still do not know if the Germans have discovered the contagious modification of Mandible yet. If they haven't, we will be in a much better position to contain the virus."

"How do you plan on doing that?" asked Vincent, his sniper rifle ready at his side. "And where is Mandible going?"

James shook his head. "If we find the blueprints for the weapon, we will know where it is going. I have only seen them once, but I know that on the bottom of the main one were the letters Uxwwhujdoh."

Conner walked in front of the man before he could take a step. "Whoa, whoa, whoa," he said, "we can't just go off and save the day. Why don't we just go home?"

Jackson put a gentle hand on Conner's left shoulder. "I don't want the lives of millions on my conscience. Neither do you, brother. We can do this. We're in the Boyd family line," he called proudly. "Our ancestors did it. So can we."

Conner breathed deeply. "All right, let's move out!"

The group headed southeast toward the heart of Germany.

Chapter 13
Uxwwhujdoh

As the men were walking, Conner ran the letters through his head carefully.

"Uxwwhujdoh," mused the man. "It must be a code or some sort of cipher."

"Who could break that code?" asked Vincent.

Jackson smiled. "Bet you even Caesar couldn't break that code!" he laughed.

The men laughed until Conner snapped his fingers. "I got it!" he said. "Well, I know what cipher this is."

The men looked at him.

"What?" asked James.

Conner could remember his history lessons now. "The Caesar Shift Cipher," he began, "was invented by Julius Caesar to communicate to his generals. The cipher worked by deciding upon a certain number to move the letter forward or backward in the alphabet. If the number was three, A would become D, which is three letters up. If it was four, A would be E, five, F. Got it?"

"Yes!" exclaimed Jackson. "There has to be a number. Give me a number!"

Vincent glanced at a code on his sniper rifle. "Try five up."

Jackson switched it, but got the answer Wzyyjwlfqj.

"Nope."

James said, "Maybe four up."

Jackson again switched it, but ended up with another scrambled set of letters, Vyxxivkepi.

"Not any better. Vyxxivkepi," attempted Jackson.

Conner nodded his head. "Try three letters back," he suggested.

Jackson switched the letters around. "What's Ruttergale?"

The former prisoner's head snapped up. "That is where I was kept before I was moved to the train," he cried. "We got it!"

Vincent smiled. "How do we get there?"

James turned toward the east and began to run. "This way," he called.

The other men followed without a single doubt to James Farion's judgment.

*   *   *   *   *

General Starr was tapping his foot nervously at his desk when a soldier came in. "Sir, we have a transmission for you. It's from our Netherlands attack group," said the soldier stiffly.

The general got up and entered the radio room, sitting down next to the radio.

"Yes, Commander Dixon? Any news?"

"Good news and bad news, sir," said the kind voice. "The good news; the Allies have taken control of the Netherlands. The bad news and good news; Vincent Stenvich's plane was sighted by one of our scouts. We couldn't risk going near it because there were tons of Germans."

There was a slight pause, and then, "The final news. One of our scouts found footprints near the crash site. They were large sizes, and four were of American make. The fifth and last one was German, but its size matches James Farion's shoe size."

General Starr leapt up. "Get your squad to follow those footprints. Once you find their owners, get a transport to send them out!"

Commander Dixon cleared his throat. "Wish me luck."

The line went dead.

General Starr clapped his hands together. His effort to find the men had not been for nothing.

*   *   *   *   *

Commander Steil struggled against his bonds for the millionth time. He couldn't break the long, tough rope that bound him to the sturdy tree.

He sat back against the scratchy bark as the breaking of twigs sounded near him. An American stepped out from behind a tree and pointed a rifle at him.

"I found someone, sir," said the soldier into his radio. "A German tied to a tree."

Steil nodded towards him. "Where is your squad?"

The man drew a long knife and sliced the rope clean away. "Behind a ways. Come on, we'll get you some food and water."

As the American turned, Commander Steil jumped forth and placed his arm against his throat. "Die, filthy scum!"

The soldier managed to break the choke, but in the struggle, lost control of his knife. Steil gripped the knife and began to force it toward his opponent's throat.

In a final move, the cruel German sliced forward, silently killing the American. After the man fell to the ground, he was raided of his shotgun, knife, and ammunition. By the time the body was found, Commander Steil had disappeared into the forest, moving deeper into Germany.

*   *   *   *   *

As dusk fell upon the forest, Conner, Jackson, James, Vincent, and Travis became tired. They made camp next to a giant hollowed tree trunk. With so much vegetation around, it was easy making a fire.

Conner stared into the crackling flames pensively. "Sometimes," he said quietly, "I wish that all of this just disappeared. The war, the virus, and the Axis itself just wither and blow off into space, with no trace left behind."

Jackson coughed several times and lay back against the wood. "Me too. I just want to go home."

James smiled. "I'll be going back to my wife with our little baby Rodger," he said wistfully.

Vincent's eyes were filled with sadness. "We might never get back," he assumed coldly.

Conner could sense a strange anger in Vincent's voice, but he decided not to say anything.

"Well, good night," announced James.

"Sleep well."

The men fell asleep next to the fire, preparing themselves for the following day.

Chapter 14
High Fever

As the sun became visible over the horizon, five planes took off from the German facility in Rhaude. Four of them were fighters, and the fifth was a large cargo transport. Looking out the window of the transport was Wilhelm von Schreider. He smiled and turned toward the soldier next to him. "So, who are you?" he asked.

The German sat casually, turning his head towards him in a friendly manner. "I am Private Cossack. Hitler told me to be your bodyguard. You must be really important then," he presumed lightly.

Wilhelm couldn't help but roll his eyes. "The nerve of him… I don't need a bodyguard."

The soldier tapped his finger to his head and smiled. "Hitler chose you to run this operation. You are important. Therefore, you need a bodyguard."

"Indeed yes," replied the German before returning to the window.

The planes banked slightly onto a southeast course as clouds began to populate the sky.

* * * * *

General Starr was sitting in the radio room with a cup of coffee when a voice entered his hearing range. It was one of his officers.

"Sir, we can't just let him fret about these people. They mean nothing to us. We need to focus on the war, not a few kids stuck in Europe."

The general froze.

Another voice entered the conversation. "I agree, Lieutenant. Something must be done about the general. What do you think, Private?"

The private spoke up. "You are traitors! Just because he cares about them doesn't mean that he should be removed from his position!"

General Starr heard a slap. "Shut up! You don't know anything. I don't care about your brother, who currently is dead in Germany. Besides, I'm sure everyone wants…"

A solid sound of fist smashing into bone rang through the man's ears. A yelp sounded, and quick footsteps left the hallway. Someone was sniffling softly outside the radio room.

The kind-hearted general got up and walked into the hallway. Standing there was Private David McCarthy. Seeing General Starr walking toward him, he wiped his eyes and stood to attention.

He smiled. "You want some coffee? It sure is good this morning!"

The man couldn't stifle a sniff. "That would be nice, sir."

General Starr ushered him to his office and poured David a hot, steaming cup of coffee.

"Cream or sugar?" he asked.

"None, please."

The general put down the cream and sugar. "Private, I am sure that your brother is all right."

He looked up. "Really?"

"Definitely," he replied. "He's got the weapons, the skill, and of course, he's pretty damn smart."

David smiled and sniffed again.

"So don't worry when people make fun of you. What would they be saying if that happened to them?" asked General Starr.

The man squirmed uncomfortably. "Did you hear all of that?" he asked.

"Yes," said General Starr. "But don't worry; you aren't in trouble. Just tell me who your two friends are."

The private clenched his teeth. "Lieutenant Brock and Captain Desmonde are the mutineers that I know of. By now, they probably have more people involved."

Starr swore under his breath and straightened in his chair, taking another sip of coffee. "What do you think? Should I sleep tonight?"

David sipped his coffee and nodded. "Sure. I'm pretty sure that they won't try to kill you. Yet, that is."

Chills went down the general's spine as he got up to walk to his room. "Thank you, Private," he said.

He smiled. "Don't worry, sir. I'll guard your room if you want."

"You do that."

The private smiled and followed the general to his room.

* * * * *

The gentle twittering of the birds eased Conner from his restful sleep. Yawning and stretching, he nudged Jackson. "Hey Jack, wake up man!"

The twin woke up with a cry. "Mark!" he called weakly.

Conner put his hand to Jackson's head. It was extremely hot. Quickly, he shoved James into Vincent, who toppled into Travis. They all woke up, rubbing their heads and cursing. Noticing Conner's look of concern, James walked over and knelt next to Jackson. "What's wrong?" he asked anxiously.

Conner grabbed James's wrist and held it to Jackson's head. His expression grew worried. "We have a major fever. Do we have any water?"

Vincent looked at his pack and pulled out a small canteen. "This is all I have."

James grabbed it, ripped a part of his shirt, and drenched it in water. Murmuring gently to Jackson, he placed it onto the twin's forehead. "There now, Jack, better isn't it?"

Jackson's eyes shut. "Fire! Death! I'm dying!"

The former prisoner poured some water into his open mouth. The twin swallowed and opened again for more.

James emptied the bottle and asked for more. Travis handed him a large canteen of water. "I salvaged it and more from our plane wreck. Try not to waste it."

Jackson whimpered. "Mandible, James, Mark, home, dying, Mandible!"

Conner gave his brother a sip of the water. He closed his mouth, stopped mumbling and shut his eyes. Soon, he was fast asleep. James continued murmuring soothingly to him, occasionally dripping water onto the ripped cloth.

"I don't think we can travel for a few days," said Vincent. "We'll have to wait for his fever to break."

James Farion looked toward him. "Mr. Stenvich, we don't have that kind of time," he said contradictorily. "Mandible could be released within a week!"

Travis shrugged his shoulders and picked up his weapons. "My suggestion is to take the kid and continue east. We need to find that virus."

Vincent shook his head, but muttered, "Fine."

Conner picked his brother up gently. "All right, let's get a move on!"

James once again took the lead as the group weaved through the forest, continuing its route east.

Chapter 15
Conflict at Home

General Starr woke up quite late. The sun was out, and the base was bustling with people. He put on his clothes, walked to his office, and poured himself a cup of hot coffee. He sprinkled a little sugar and a dash of cream into it and sipped it. Nodding his head in satisfaction, he walked to the radio room. The officer on duty approached him. "Sir, we have a call from Commander Dixon, sir!"

The general saluted him appreciatively. "Thank you." He took the radio from the man's hands. "Commander, what's the scoop?"

"Well, one of our soldiers was found, dead. Next to him was a bunch of cut ropes. It looks like he untied someone's bonds, and managed to get killed. It was a clean knife cut. The only radio contact we had with the soldier was him saying that he had found a German tied to a tree. We found the body this morning. Looks as if he has been dead for the whole night. He was raided of his supplies as well," announced Commander Dixon. "I think we have a very skilled assassin on our hands."

General Starr sat down in a chair. "Any news about the footprints you found?"

Commander Dixon's voice grew bleak. "I think one of them is dead."

The general smote his forehead. "How?"

"Well," he recalled, "our scout followed the footsteps to a camp. One of the sets of American shoes disappeared when they left. That coupled with the heavier set of prints for one of the men means that the body is being carried."

"What if one of them broke their legs?" asked General Starr anxiously.

"We see no evidence of that, sir. I am extremely sorry," replied the kind voice. "We haven't ruled out sickness, though. I'll keep you posted."

The voice paused for a moment. "Sir?"

General Starr managed to say, "Yes, Commander. Keep me posted."

He cut the connection and buried his face in his hands. "Save them, Lord!" he called shakily.

*   *   *   *   *

The plane had been flying for about an hour when they began their descent. With a slight bump, the transport touched down, and its fighter escorts curled around and flew until they were out of sight.

The transport stopped and the doors were opened. Wilhelm von Schreider jumped out and walked up to the pilot, who had opened his door and was powering down.

"Get someone to take the cargo to the storage room. I want ten guards on it," he rapped.

"Yes, sir!" called the pilot as he got out and walked toward the main building.

Wilhelm turned and went the opposite way, heading toward another large building with a strange circular tube on top. Private Cossack followed without a word.

*   *   *   *   *

The group had been traveling for only an hour when Conner stopped. "I can't hold him anymore!" he called anxiously.

James groaned and sat down. "We're almost out of the forest!"

He laid Jackson on the ground gently. "We need to wait."

Vincent and Travis sat next to Conner. "All right," relented the soldier. "We'll rest for a bit."

The group sat in silence for a moment.

"Well?" asked Travis.

Conner put a hand to his brother's forehead. "It is all sweaty," he replied. "He may have broken his fever."

Jackson's eyes snapped open. "Hey, guys."

James moved over next to him. "Hey, how do you feel?"
"Okay."
"Are you ready to move out?" he asked.
Jackson shook his head and sat up. "Where are we?"
James looked around. "We're still in the forest. It looks like we'll be out of here in a few hours."
He stood up shakily. "I'm ready, gentlemen. Let's move out!"
The group departed again, talking as they went.

* * * * *

Commander Steil was walking through the forest when he heard voices behind him.
"Any footprints?"
"The group is over here. Looks like one of them is back," said one of the voices. "Yeah, it's the same footprint."
Commander Steil hid behind a tree an instant before the two American scouts pushed aside the underbrush and came into the small clearing.
"We have one set over here. It's fresh. We must've just missed this dude."
The first American glanced at the footprint. "This must be only a minute old!" he exclaimed. "Radio back to base."
The German heard a beep.
"We have fresh footprints with the old ones. They are about a minute old and counting. Get five men over here now. We need…"
Commander Steil made his move. He crept up to the man and slit his throat.
"Sir?" asked the voice over the radio.
The other American picked up the radio. "We've been attacked! Come in now!"
The handle of the shotgun slammed into the man's forehead. He still was upright. He took out a rifle and aimed it at the commander's forehead.

68

"Get down!" yelled the scout.

Commander Steil let himself fall to the ground.

"Surrender all of your weapons!"

The German handed him the shotgun.

"The knife?"

He made to hand it over, but threw it at the American's head. The man twisted, and the knife flew over him. "Nice try, German," said the soldier.

As the soldier turned to get the knife, Commander Steil looked to the left. He could see three German soldiers lying prone in front of him.

One of them got up. "Freeze!" he called.

The American turned around and was roughly tied up. "We'll win this war!" he yelled. All he received was a slap as the men ran away, taking him with them.

*　　*　　*　　*　　*

General Starr was pacing around the radio room when an officer grabbed the radio. "Sir, we are getting a transmission from Commander Dixon!"

He took the radio quickly and held it to his ear. "What's happening over there?" he asked.

"Well," said Commander Dixon, "one of our men was captured by a few Germans. We don't know where he is. The good part is the footsteps for one of the men came back. The strange thing is that the men who took our scout are following the men you are trying to find. They are moving rather quickly, so we can't intercept them before they reach your guys."

General Starr shrugged. "Well done. I look forward to hearing from you soon!"

The line disconnected.

He rubbed his temples and sat in a chair as the officer looked at him with concern. "Are you all right, sir?"

"Yes," grunted the general. "Oh, can you send for Lieutenant Brock and Captain Desmonde? Tell them to meet me in my office."

The officer nodded and left the room as General Starr got up and walked to his office.

* * * * *

"Good morning, sir!" called a voice.

Wilhelm von Schreider pushed through the doors. "Patch me in to Hitler now!"

The guard pulled a radio from his belt and handed it to him. "We got him on now."

"Ah, Adolf!" laughed Wilhelm. "How are you?"

"Enough of the pleasantries. Where is it?" cried the voice.

"I have it now," replied Wilhelm. "Where do you want me to go with it?"

"Move the cargo to the place we talked about. Meet me there at midday tomorrow."

"I understand, sir," said Wilhelm. "See you there."

The line went dead.

Chapter 16
Rendezvous Point

After a few hours of travel, the forest had begun to thin and disappear. As the final rows of trees came into view, Conner ordered a rest. Jackson was breathing extremely hard, and his head was rather warm.

"You know," said James. "I just remembered something. A way we could get home."

Conner took the canteen from Travis gratefully and sipped at it. "What?"

"When I was imprisoned," began the man, "I was asked over and over again where the plans were. The plans were in the Netherlands, with a man named Commander Dixon. The plans were for a massive strike against the Germans. And he is leading Operation Windbreaker, as it is called."

"The Netherlands aren't far from here, so presumably, they have begun their quiet march east. Once we stop Mandible, we will have an escape route. All we need to do is go west."

"Now, the attack will take place about two weeks from now. It will hit Germany at Berlin and Bremen, two of the best protected cities in this country. Unfortunately, someone leaked that there would be an attack on Germany to a man named Commander Steil."

"That's right," said a quiet voice. James turned to see Commander Steil leaning against a tree. Vincent raised his sniper rifle and Travis aimed his rifle at the German. Just as Vincent pulled the trigger, a soldier jumped from behind a tree and smacked the two both on the head, knocking them out. The bullet glanced off a tree and disappeared from sight.

Jackson dove for Travis's gun, but another two Germans appeared from behind their comrade and hauled him to his feet. A quick punch sent him flying into a tree, unconscious. Enraged, Conner ran at Commander Steil, who raised his shotgun. He fired, but the twin contorted away from the shot and dove toward the German. They both went down and began to roll down a hill. Anchoring himself to a tree, Commander Steil was able to draw his knife. He sliced at Conner and the knife plunged into a piece of wood that the American was holding. Smiling, Conner took out the knife, threw it away, and swung at him with the thick branch. Just in time, the German picked up another branch and parried the blow. In a fatal move, he glanced at the knife and pushed Conner over it.

Conner cried out in pain and pulled the knife from his back. With skill born from anger, he threw the knife at Commander Steil.

The knife moved in almost slow motion as it buried itself in the German's heart.

A choking sound emanated from him, and he fell to his knees. Clutching at the knife in his chest, he fell to the ground, dead.

Shaking all over, Conner took his shotgun, supplies, and with a disgusted look on his face, the knife. Wiping the knife on Commander Steil's shirt, he placed it into his belt.

He loaded the shotgun and ran up the hill. The Germans were standing there.

"Hey!" yelled Conner. The men looked up as the shotgun bullets went home. They slumped over each other and were motionless.

"James, Jackson, Vincent, Travis! Are you all right?" he asked.

"Yeah," called James weakly. "They're all out except me!"

A cry permeated the air.

"What the hell was that?" asked Conner.

"I'm trapped!" called a voice. "I am an American. The Germans got me, but they left."

Conner tossed Travis's rifle to James and ran into the forest.

"Where are you?" he called.

"Over here!" A bloody hand gestured from behind a tree.

Conner ran to the man and patted his head. "Are you all right, sir?" he asked.

"Forget 'sir'," admonished the man. "Let's get out of this horrible forest. Untie my legs and hands, please!"

Conner sliced the rope away. "We need to wake up the rest of our men. Come on."

The men walked back to the encampment, nursing their wounds.

* * * * *

General Starr sat at his desk, musing over some papers. The door opened loudly and two men walked in.

"Ah, Lieutenant Brock, Captain Desmonde," he said invitingly. The men sat down silently.

"Why must you talk to us?" asked the lieutenant. "Sir?" he added quickly.

The general smiled. "I think you know."

One of Captain Desmonde's hands began to inch below the table. "Well," he said. "We don't, sir."

"Captain, it seems as if you two are planning a mutiny," he said coolly. "Coffee, anyone?"

The men shifted in their chairs. "Why would we mutiny?" asked Lieutenant Brock. "And I wouldn't mind coffee."

"You tell me!"

Suddenly, the captain's hand came up. In it was a knife.

"You are going too far!" yelled General Starr.

Captain Desmonde jumped over the general's desk and sliced down.

A gasp sounded from behind them. Turning, Lieutenant Brock saw the private.

"Traitors deserve to die!" he yelled as he removed a knife from his belt. With a desperate stroke, he flung the knife toward the lieutenant. With a gurgle, the man slumped to the ground, the knife protruding from his neck. Not bothering to remove the knife from the dead mutineer, he jumped forward and punched Captain Desmonde once. The man fell to the floor. With tears running down his cheeks, David began to choke him.

"Die… you… filthy… scum!"

The captain writhed and writhed, but the angry soldier continued his relentless grip. With a final squeeze, the thrashing ended.

General Starr could only hear the voices of the officers beginning to enter the room and the sobbing of the wretched private as his vision faded to darkness.

*   *   *   *   *

Wilhelm watched as the sky began to grow dark. It was silent except for the rustling of the leaves on the trees.

"Sir?" asked Private Cossack, who was standing behind him.

"Yes, Private?

"When are we to leave?"

Wilhelm closed his eyes and felt the cool breeze ruffle his hair. "Prepare the ship. It is just us this time. Leave the pilot here."

"Yes, sir." The private walked away.

Chapter 17
Midnight Flight

The sun had just set when the group began to move again. Jackson, Travis, and Vincent had all regained their consciousness quickly.

As they walked through the final row of trees, James asked, "Did you kill him, Conner?"

"Yes."

"Well done," he congratulated. "This guy was one pain in the butt. He was my interrogator when I was in prison in Ruttergale. He was cruel."

The men passed the final row of trees and entered a meadow.

"How far to Ruttergale?" asked Vincent coldly.

James shrugged. "I don't know. All I know is that it is this way."

"Stop!"

The men stopped and looked at Conner. Shaking, he pointed to a small metal object sticking up from the ground. "This is a mine. And there probably is a field full of them. Exercise extreme caution and go back.

The men gingerly stepped back to the trees. "Now what?" Travis asked.

Vincent's well-trained eyes swept over the meadow. "If we throw grenades into our path, we might be able to clear the mines. Besides, this meadow is rather small. We should be able to get across with the grenades that we have."

Travis unhooked a grenade from his belt and threw it hard toward the center of the meadow. It detonated and sent tall stalks of grain everywhere, leaving a bare spot.

"All right, Vincent. Your turn."

Travis handed the assassin a grenade, and he expertly tossed it to about halfway to the bare spot. It exploded, leaving another bare spot on the ground.

"We only have three left. Go to the first spot," called James.

The men jumped to the closest spot one by one. Another grenade created a path to the halfway point. They walked over to the center of the meadow.

Travis handed a grenade to Conner. He pulled the pin and spiked it hard against the ground.

It bounced several times. Each time, a mine exploded next to it. Finally, it detonated with a bang, destroying the final mine and leaving a clear path to the other side of the meadow.

Laughing, James clapped Conner on the back. "How did you do that?" he asked.

"I don't know," replied the twin. "Let's go."

The men crossed the meadow and reached a road. A sign at the side indicated that Ruttergale was only a mile away.

"Let's go."

The men began to walk down the road, with only the moon to light their path.

* * * * *

"General Starr!" called a voice. "General Starr! Can you hear me?"

The general's eyes snapped open. A young medic wearing white came into his blurry vision. "Sir, can you hear me?" he asked again.

"Yes," the general croaked. His chest hurt every time he took a breath. "What… happened?"

"Captain Desmonde stabbed you in the chest. Consider yourself lucky, because if that knife had been a centimeter closer to your heart, it would have punctured one of your main arteries. You would've died," The man smiled and patted him on the head. "How are you feeling, sir? Better?"

"Food!" he whispered.

"You can't have anything for a few hours. But just wait. You'll get some food soon," replied the man. "Oh, someone wants to see you."

The medic walked away.

General Starr's vision sharpened as Private McCarthy shuffled into the room and sat down next to him. Burying his head into his hands, he sobbed. "I failed to protect you!"

"It's okay," soothed the general. "I'm alive."

"I know!" he cried. "But if you had been killed…"

"Well, I wasn't," said the general. "Help me sit up, please."

The private got up, wiped his eyes with his sleeve, and propped him up on the pillows.

"How long have I been out?"

"Not long, maybe a few hours."

"What happened to the mutineers?"

"I killed them," replied the private, his voice shaking. "I stabbed Brock in the neck and choked Desmonde with my bare hands."

General Starr frowned. "And who is taking my place?"

"No one yet, sir. The whole place is in chaos after that fiasco." David rolled his eyes.

The general spoke almost immediately. "I want you to take my place."

David placed a hand on his chest. "Me?"

"Yes. You are the only one who will continue my work to find those men in Germany."

The private was speechless.

General Starr reached into his pocket and removed a key. "Use this to get to my files. You may use my office if you wish. Good luck, Private."

Private McCarthy took the key and smiled. "Thank you, General." He left the room at a brisk pace.

*　*　*　*　*

Wilhelm von Schreider and Private Cossack sat in the cockpit of the transport. They had taken off at about midnight, and they had been in the air for a few hours already.

"Well?" asked Private Cossack. "Where are we going?"

"A small city built next to a lake. That's all I can tell you right now."

The private nodded and turned toward the window as Wilhelm banked the plane slightly to the north. "Ah, the landing strip!" he called. "Private Cossack, radio them our position."

As the man talked to the control center, Wilhelm maneuvered the plane to a smooth landing. It rolled to a stop, and taxied slowly toward the control center. He stopped the plane and powered it down. "Private, tell them that this is the man who needs to see Adolf Hitler."

Private Cossack nodded and said, "Sir, this man must see Hitler."

The voice on the other end disconnected and a man came out of the central building. He was surrounded by several guards.

"Wilhelm!" called the man. "Excellent, right on schedule!"

The two men opened the plane doors and jumped out. "Ah, Hitler! We have it. So, where are we going now?"

"We plan on going east a few miles to the main facility. There, we will build the bomb," replied Adolf with a wide grin on his face.

"Are the trucks ready?" asked Wilhelm.

Adolf pointed to the main building. "We have a garage in there. Let's move the boxes onto the trucks. Let's go, let's go!"

The guards hastily placed their weapons on the ground and began to move the boxes.

"All better. Now, let's go inside."

*   *   *   *   *

After several hours, the sun peeked over the horizon, and the men stopped. Weary from the night's walk, they sat down against an old fence and relaxed.

"Ruttergale is just ahead," gasped Jackson.

The man who had just joined them smiled. "Yeah. And I forgot to tell you my name. It's Steven."

James proffered two rifles and tossed them to Jackson and Steven. "You'll need those. I already have my own." He patted the barrel of the rifle sitting on his lap.

"So, what is the plan?" asked Conner.

Vincent raised his sniper rifle and looked through the scope toward the city ahead. "There are two guards on the road and three in the guard post. Do you want me to take them out?"

Travis grumbled, "No. They'll sound the alarm before you kill them all."

"There has to be another way into the city!" exclaimed James. "But how?"

"We have to storm it," said Jackson.

James was shaking his head. "No, Mandible isn't here."

Vincent turned his head toward him, a strange look on his face. "How do you know?"

"They would've moved it."

"Hey, what is that?" asked Conner.

A large caravan of vehicles was visible down the road. "Run for cover!" called James, and the men jumped into the thick reeds at the side of the road.

As the men waited, Conner counted the vehicles. As he peered through the reeds, trying to look through the windshield of the middle car, he saw a strikingly familiar face.

"Adolf Hitler?" he said to himself.

James put a hand over his mouth. "We know. Shut up!"

The cars passed, and the men stood up. "What should we do?" asked Jackson.

The former British soldier gazed pensively at the cars. "Follow them."

Chapter 18
Arrival

Private David McCarthy was seated at General Starr's desk when three captains came in. "Someone wishes to speak with you," one said.

He got up and left the office. A tall man was standing in front of him. "Ah, *Private* McCarthy. What gives you permission to assume control of this base?"

"General Starr," replied the private, unfazed. "And who are you?"

"My name is Colonel Armani. I am second in command of this base," he rapped, "so I am in charge here."

David was rather intimidated by this towering figure, but he did not back down. "No, *sir*, I am in charge! General Starr placed me in command of this base, so I will do what he says until he recovers! Do you understand me?" he yelled angrily.

Armani looked at his feet and saluted. "Yes, sir," he chirped quietly, and walked away.

Private McCarthy looked after him, his eyes dark.

* * * * *

The trucks had been moving steadily for a while when they finally began to slow down. Wilhelm raised his head and looked out the windshield. Ahead of them was the facility.

It was a big operation. A large, cylindrical building with a flat roof was encircled by six smaller structures. Around those was a perimeter fence, complete with guard posts and a barbed wire top. The only gate was heavily guarded with several soldiers and a triple-lock.

The truck that Wilhelm was in stopped, and a German opened the door silently and gestured toward the gate.

With a loud screech, it opened. Wilhelm smiled and walked through. Immediately after him, the trucks were driven through toward the main building. He stood against the wall, watching the Germans closing the gate.

"Magnificent, isn't it, Wilhelm?" called a voice.

He turned to see Adolf. "Yes, indeed!"

"When do you think it will be ready?"

"Two to three days, at the most," von Schreider replied. "Then, we will achieve victory!"

* * * * *

"How much farther do we have to walk?" Conner asked strenuously. There had been no way of passing through the city, so they had decided that they would have to go all the way around.

"We don't know," replied James unhappily. "Hopefully, the Germans are leading us directly to the weapon."

Jackson stumbled, but Steven gripped his arm firmly and hauled him back onto his feet. "Easy there," he grunted. "What are you guys doing anyway?"

James wiped his brow. "We are trying to find a virus called Mandible. If the Germans use it correctly, they could kill the entire United States population."

"Well, that's new!" he said cheerfully. "So how are you going to stop this virus?"

Travis grimaced as his foot fell into a puddle. "No clue."

Jackson looked ahead. "Hey, look! It's the road!"

Conner smiled. "Excellent. Now, we can get our bearings."

They reached the road. Vincent knelt down and traced his finger over a small skid mark. "They are on this road, and they are going this way. All we need to do is to catch up to them," he said softly.

Steven glanced at the skid mark, and then looked up toward the horizon. "It must be pretty far, because I don't see any trucks."

"Water, anyone?" asked Travis.

They all muttered their thanks and took a brief sip from his canteen.

"Okay, let's go. We need to follow these tracks," said James.

The group began to move again, growing ever closer to their destination.

*   *   *   *   *

An officer ran through the hallway as fast as he could, a radio in his hand. "Private, Private McCarthy! It's for you."

David got up from his chair and entered the hallway. "Sir, what's the hurry?"

"It's Commander Dixon, sir!"

He took the radio. "Commander Dixon, what is new on the battlefront?"

"What do you want first; the good news or the bad news?" the voice asked.

"Either."

"Well, I heard about the mutiny," said Commander Dixon, "it's too bad. How is he doing?"

"All right," replied the private.

"I'll start with the bad news. We found several bodies near the edge of the Rhaude Forest. Fortunately, your guys aren't among the dead."

"And?"

"The good news is that we have checked our maps in correspondence to the route of the men, and we have discovered that they are following a road now. However, the tracks veered right off the road before Ruttergale, so we presume that they are circling the city to find the road again. So, we can make an educated guess as to where they are going."

"Where?"

A sigh emanated from the radio. "We have noticed that the road makes a strange move, as if it is moving around something. This gives us the idea that the men are moving toward some sort of building that the Germans didn't want to put on the map."

"Can you get a helicopter out there?"

"Not now, but when we attack Ruttergale, we will probably find a helicopter."

"Excellent, thank you," exclaimed the private.
The line disconnected.

*   *   *   *   *

The group finally stopped as the sun began to come down. They lay down at the side of the road and fell asleep, tired from their long march.

Chapter 19
Target in Sight

Wilhelm woke up sitting against a cold wall. His knee crackled painfully as he got up.

Moving his hands upward, he noticed that he had drawn the beautiful sword in his sleep. Rubbing his eyes, he replaced it in his sheath. He then found the door and left the room.

He entered the bitterly cold night air outside. He took a deep breath and stood there stupidly. He looked around. A single guard stood on duty several yards away, with a hot cup of coffee in his hand. Desperate for a source of warmth, he walked over to the man.

"Where can I find the coffee?" he asked.

The guard turned stiffly and pointed at the door of the main building. "The first room, sir," he replied coldly.

Without another word, Wilhelm walked to the door, pulled it open, and entered swiftly, shutting the door behind him.

There were several tables in the room, but only one was occupied. Adolf and Private Cossack were sitting on either end of an empty chair, both holding coffees.

"Ah, Wilhelm!" called Adolf, proffering his coffee cup and motioning to the thermos and the cups in the middle of the table. "Come on, why don't you have a drink?"

Wilhelm didn't say a word as he sat down and poured himself some coffee. For several moments, it was silent. Private Cossack finally spoke. "Sir," he said quietly, addressing the new arrival, "what will you do if this doesn't work?"

Wilhelm took a brief sip of the coffee. "I'll take a helicopter out of here."

"But what about the virus? You're not just going to leave it there! What they could do with it..." His voice trailed off.

"The *Americans* don't know anything about this. Germany is impenetrable, particularly here," countered Wilhelm fiercely.

Adolf took a final draught of his coffee, set his cup down, and got up. "Well, gentlemen, that will be all. I will leave the base in the morning and leave Wilhelm to finish the job. I will watch the rockets from my bunker in Berlin."

He walked out of the room, leaving a smoky fragrance in his wake.

Private Cossack looked up and cleared his throat. "Well," he said quietly, "I should go back to my room."

"Where is my room?" he asked his bodyguard quietly.

"You're in a room next to mine. I'll show you."

The two left the room without another word.

*   *   *   *   *

Commander Dixon watched as the attack group opened Ruttergale's gates. "Move in, soldiers!" he called.

The troops poured into the city, yelling loudly. The German guards looked up, alarmed. Commander Dixon raised a hand, and the snipers around him fired their rifles in unison. The guards went down easily. The first line of defense was eliminated in a matter of seconds.

However, one strong spot existed. A large field was in the middle of the city, covered with mines. A group of pillboxes surrounded the small domed structure in the middle. And next to the building was the helicopter that they needed.

"We need air support to take out this stronghold, sir," buzzed the radio.

Commander Dixon shut his eyes. A strange picture came to his memory. "Hey, throw your grenades into the field."

"Yes, sir!"

A large banging was heard in the city, and then an exhilarated voice came over the radio. "The machine guns are disabled! Forward! Attack!"

The soldiers yelled victoriously and ran over the path that their grenades had created. The final German group was annihilated in less than a minute.

"Sir, we have the helicopter! Mission accomplished!"

Commander Dixon stepped forward, with a rifle in his hands and a curved saber in its sheath at his waist. "Prepare the helicopter for takeoff. We must help our men!"

*　　*　　*　　*　　*

The group woke up near noontime and began their march again. The tire tracks were becoming more recent as they walked.

Conner stopped for a moment and sat down. "We can't continue much longer like this."

The group hadn't eaten for days, and their water was almost gone.

Jackson helped his brother up. "There has to be some food nearby!"

James grunted and pointed ahead. The group looked ahead and quickly hid in the brush next to the road.

"It's a bunch of Germans," whispered Conner. "They outnumber us two to one."

James smiled. "Mandible must be here!"

"And they have food!" said Travis hoarsely.

Vincent's cold eyes blinked once. "I will snipe them. Steven and Travis, you'll need to provide cover fire to get their heads down. Conner, move up and fire at them from the ridge."

Vincent loaded his weapon loudly, and before any heads could turn, he fired his sniper rifle straight into the pack of Germans.

Two Germans fell, and another clutched his arm tightly. Travis and Steven unloaded a barrage of gunfire onto the Germans, killing four. The injured one picked up a rifle, only to get whapped over the head with Conner's shotgun. The remaining five began to run away. Conner cried out. "Stop them!"

Steven sprinted after the Germans. He fired four shots, bringing down four of the remaining Germans. He reloaded as he ran and aimed at the last one.

Almost in slow motion, the German turned around and fired one solitary shot. Steven took the full force of the bullet in his chest and fell to the ground.

Vincent kept his cool and ran forward. He aimed at the fleeing figure and pulled the trigger.

A loud cry was heard, and then silence took over the road.

Conner was at Steven's side. No tears went down his angry face. "They'll pay for this!"

* * * * *

Private McCarthy walked into General Starr's room. He smiled at the sight of his old friend. "So, how are you doing?"

Starr smiled. "Better. Any news?"

David told the general about the strange curve in the road.

"Well," mused the general, "it seems as if the Germans are hiding a building. What else would it be?"

"So, where are the men?" he asked.

"They just passed Ruttergale. They are following that same road that curves in a strange manner," the private replied.

"Interesting. They must be following someone."

Private McCarthy perked up. "They must be following the head of the building or base! There's a lead!"

He took a radio from his belt. "Commander Dixon, do you copy?"

"Yes, sir. What do you need?"

"General Starr and I have a hunch. We think that there is a base at the road turn and that the men are following the head of the base. Get that helicopter and give them some support!"

Commander Dixon laughed. "We just got one. All right, all forces move out!"

The line disconnected.

"You're making a real bet here," General Starr warned. "However, I think you may be right."

* * * * *

The group had begun to march again nearly an hour before. They were refreshed, thanks to the food that had been stuffed into the Germans' packs. However, they hardly spoke a word. Steven had just been shot and killed at the hands of the Germans. Everyone's knuckles were white with anger.

James shuffled to a stop and glanced at the horizon. He could barely see a building with a cylindrical shape in the distance. "Gentlemen, our target is in sight!"

Chapter 20
Operation Windbreaker

Wilhelm von Schreider woke up to light flooding the room. He got out of his rickety bed and stood up. Most of the windows were open to let in the late morning sunlight. Grunting, he dressed in his dark German uniform and left the room.

He left the building to see several workers bustling about. Smiling, he walked over to a young officer. "Where are we on the construction?"

"The weapon will be finished by midnight. However, we need to fill it with the virus, so that will take until the morning," he replied sharply.

Wilhelm patted him on the back. "Could you show me the construction?"

The officer nodded curtly and walked stiffly to the stairs that encircled the building. "Follow me, sir," he said.

Von Schreider was almost surprised when they reached the top of the building. The weapon dwarfed them, reaching a height of nearly one hundred meters. However, his eyes were focused on the network of catwalks that extended outward from the roof, leading to canisters of Mandible that were being emptied into the missile by long steel pipes.

"Well, there you have it!" called the officer as Wilhelm took a step onto one of the catwalks. "Oh, and the best part. Let me show you!"

Wilhelm was ushered down a narrow catwalk into a small room on one of the small platforms. "When the missile is ready, you will be here," said the officer. "Missile control buttons, defense mechanisms; the entire deal. Some of these defenses are rather interesting…"

Wilhelm sat at the ebony desk in the dark room and felt the buttons. A small grey button labeled "Catwalks" stood out to him. He pointed to it. "What does this one do?"

"That, sir, retracts the catwalk rails. If intruders come and are leaning against the rail, that is a good button to press. The rail simply falls away."

Wilhelm closed his eyes. "Interesting, very interesting!"

* * * * *

Commander Dixon watched as his forces began to move. He shook his head and turned to his generals. "We aren't moving fast enough! How are we supposed to move in the entire force, position it in time to intercept the men, and complete the invasion of Bremen and Berlin?"

A young sniper who was standing at his side spoke quietly. "It's impossible, sir, unless we get the entire Air Force over here. Operation Windbreaker must be continued as quickly as possible."

The generals agreed solemnly. "We must simply hope that we reach them fast enough to ensure their safety. Based on their eastward movement, they must be after something. A quite powerful something."

Commander Dixon nodded gravely and spoke into the radio. "Is the helicopter almost ready?"

"Yes, sir," buzzed the radio. "Just give us a couple hours."

The man buried his face into his hands as the sun sunk below the horizon.

* * * * *

Wilhelm von Schreider had fallen asleep in the control room when a sharp nudge awoke him. He glanced up into the officer's eyes. "The weapon is ready. We are filling the main canisters now."

The German rubbed his eyes blearily. "What time is it?"

"An hour past midnight, sir," replied the officer. "Come."

The two walked out of the room onto the main platform. A bright floodlight bathed the tall weapon with whiteness.

"Excellent!" called Wilhelm. "Hurrah!"

A swarm of mechanics made its way to the main tanks of Mandible. Silently, they towed them away. Only three supplemental tanks remained.

"We are going to be finished by morning, but we will need to wait until noon so the weapon reaches the United States at midnight and so the lock system on the missile will deactivate," said the officer proudly.

Wilhelm nodded, pleased. "Well done. I want the main personnel to ready the trucks now. They will leave after breakfast. The guards will stay until the weapon is launched, and we will escape in the remaining trucks. Got that?"

"Yes, sir!" replied the officer curtly as he swiveled on the heel of his boot and walked away toward the stairs.

*   *   *   *   *

The group walked well through the night, proceeding through midnight without a rest. Finally, Conner collapsed at the side of the road, gasping for breath. The other men did the same, rolling to the side of the road and glancing at the horizon.

"We'd better get some rest," called Jackson.

Many mutterings of satisfaction emanated from the group and they began to fall asleep. One by one, they began to snore gently.

However, hardly a second before Conner's eyes shut, a large object lit up in the distance. He covered his eyes briefly, and squinted at it.

It was a missile.

"Guys, wake up!"

The men woke up immediately. "What?" muttered Jackson, but his mouth dropped when his eyes turned to the gigantic missile in the distance.

James Farion looked at it in awe. "This is it. Mandible is here."

Chapter 21
Ready for Launch

Wilhelm awoke from his chair abruptly. Straightening his back, he stood up carefully. He rubbed his forehead and walked to the main platform.

The weapon was entirely finished. The sun had risen completely over the horizon, and the cloudless day made launch conditions perfect. Looking over the rail, he could see a large line of trucks making their way east. He smiled and began to survey the defenses. He knew that thirty guards were on the premises, but he wanted to see if there were any weak spots around the perimeter. Seeing none, he watched as a young guard sprinted up the metal stairs. "Sir, I brought you some breakfast. Fresh Italian croissants and a fresh orange with some good old black coffee, sir."

Wilhelm nodded thankfully and accepted the tray the soldier bore. "Sounds great," he said enthusiastically. "Are the trucks ready?"

"Yes, sir."

"Are the guards ready to leave?"

"Yes, sir."

"How much longer until noon?"

"We have three hours, sir."

Wilhelm patted the surprised guard on the shoulder. "Tell Private Cossack that I wish to see him."

The man nodded and ran down the stairs quickly.

Wilhelm laid a hand to the side of the missile and laughed evilly. "No one can stop me now! No one!"

* * * * *

Private David McCarthy was sitting next to General Starr's bed when a young officer ran in. "Sir, it is Commander Dixon."

He took it and held it to his ear. "What's happening?"

"We took Ruttergale and we got a helicopter. We are moving out. It is morning, and the helicopter won't be ready until late morning, so we can't intercept your men in time. However, we might get to them a few minutes after noon," replied Commander Dixon. "Our main force is focusing on eliminating Bremen. Our strike team will move onto your guys and remove them from the area."

Private McCarthy grunted. "Anything else?" he asked.

"Nope. I'll radio you when I get some more information."

The line disconnected.

General Starr lay pensively. "I know those men; they won't turn away from whatever they are against."

David nodded. "I agree, but will that be what destroys them?"

"That's what we are to find out," replied the general.

*   *   *   *   *

Commander Dixon watched as his mechanics worked on the helicopter. One of them turned and walked over to him. "Sir, the engine is nearly fixed. We'll just need to equip her with some ammo and fill her up with some gas, and she'll be ready for combat, sir," he said proudly.

He smiled and dismissed the mechanic. He turned to one of his officers. "Get our best riflemen, snipers, and machine gunners together and prepare them for the flight," he ordered.

The officer glanced at him. "Those men seem pretty important, sir. I'd go to rescue them."

Commander Dixon gazed at the horizon pensively. His hand caressed the hilt of the curved sword at his side. "You're right. I must go."

*   *   *   *   *

After a sleepless night, the group began to march toward the building again. When it was less than three hundred yards away, they hid behind a row of bushes.

"So, what's the plan?" asked Conner expectantly.

"They have ten guards at the gate, making it impassable. However, the perimeter seems weak…"

Vincent's voice trailed off when one of the guards patrolling the perimeter turned in their direction.

"Now what?" Jackson rasped quietly.

The assassin raised his sniper rifle, raising a ruckus of whispers.

"That'll get their attention!" whispered James fiercely.

"I'll rush the wall. You guys move through the gate," said Vincent valiantly. "Move!"

The men crouched as Vincent ran from the bushes and fired a shot. The patrol was thrown backward into the wall, dead. Just as the clever assassin had predicted, the gate opened, allowing five of the guards through. Four guards knelt on the roof of one of the cylindrical buildings and began firing rifle shots at him. However, Vincent had the advantage of a sniper rifle. He drilled four bullets home, knocking one of the Germans from the building with a cry. However, the five gate guards had gotten too close for his main weapon to be an advantage. In desperation, Vincent unhooked the small pistol from his belt and fired three times. Two of the soldiers fell. However, the assassin knew that he couldn't survive the barrage for long. Three bullets slammed into his chest and he stood for a moment, looking down at his chest, and fell to the ground. None of the guards noticed that the gun was still in his hand until too late.

Bam! Bam! Bam! The trigger pulled three times, killing all three of the remaining guards. Smiling, Vincent got up, uninjured, pulling the small bark bits from his chest.

Conner and the rest of the group ran cautiously to the main gate. Peeking around the corner, they saw the five soldiers. Four were standard infantry, but one of them manned a heavy machine gun.

James groaned softly. "If only we had sniper rifles."

Travis gripped his gun hard and made a silent prayer. "Hold on."

He leaned against the wall, held his rifle out in view of the soldiers, and fired several random shots. To his surprise, the machine gunner toppled over with a loud cry.

With a yell, the group ran into the base. Three of the guards went down easily, and the other shot himself in the head, causing an ugly spray of blood and guts.

Conner grimaced. "Ugh."

Travis reloaded his weapon rapidly and patted Conner on the back. "It's okay. We're in."

Chapter 22
Infiltration

"Sir, we're done. The helicopter is ready."

Commander Dixon smiled and patted the shoulder of the mechanic he was speaking to. "Well done. Now, strike team, board the helicopter."

The team boarded the helicopter as the sun drew ever closer to the top of the sky.

* * * * *

Wilhelm groaned as gunshots began to sound from the main gate. "What's happening?" he asked.

Private Cossack looked down at the gate. "We are under attack!"

"Get the rest of the guards up here!" he yelled. "I need them to hold whoever this is off until the bomb is launched. Do we have a helicopter?"

"No, sir."

"When is the bomb to be launched?"

Private Cossack walked to the missile and knelt next to a small timer. "We've got fifteen minutes until launch."

* * * * *

Private McCarthy's radio buzzed loudly. "Yes?" he asked.

The muffled voice of Commander Dixon came over the radio. "The helicopter is in the air," he called.

"Good!" exclaimed the private. "What else?"

"Two things. The base that you were talking about…"

"What about the base?"

Fear was clearly etched in Commander Dixon's voice. "We see… we see…"

"What, sir?

"We see… a gigantic missile pointed straight at the United States."

The radio thudded to the floor.

"General Starr! General Starr!" he yelled.

"What?" asked Starr quietly as David skidded as he stopped in his room.

Private McCarthy took a moment to gather his senses. "Commander Dixon said… said that he sees… a giant missile pointed straight at… us!"

General Starr perked up in fear. "Where the hell did that come from? Why didn't our guys pick it up before?"

Private McCarthy let an exasperated breath escape his lungs. "I don't know."

General Starr closed his eyes. "Help me out of bed, McCarthy."

The astonished private helped the injured general out of bed.

Immediately, the general reached for the bed in support, but with a strange cry, pulled his hand away. He stood to his full height. "I've made a lot of mistakes in life, but I am not going to make a mistake that will cost the lives of everyone in this country. My wife and my children left me because of my mistakes. And I will not lie in bed when my country is in peril! I, General Edison Starr, will not let anyone mess with my country! Private, I'm back in business. Get me my uniform and give me that radio!"

* * * * *

Conner surveyed the area. The main building was up ahead, and he could see two men standing next to the missile. He could also see sixteen guards running up the spiral stairs that encircled the building. He took a few shots at them, and one of the guards toppled over the side of the rail and fell to the ground. A small noise was heard behind them, and they turned to see Vincent holding his sniper rifle. "Hey guys. It worked, didn't it?"

Jackson gave him a bear hug. "Nice job, Vincent."

He returned the favor and glanced at the top of the building. "Too bad. I only have one bullet left in my rifle."

Conner picked a rifle that had been dropped by one of the dead Germans and tossed it to him. "There you go," he said. "Use your final shot wisely."

Vincent slung the sniper rifle over his back. "I'll save it."

"Good idea. So, what do we do to get up there?" asked James.

Travis looked at the building next to him, and then looked at the catwalks overhead. "Get in here."

The men busted open the door to the building and entered it. A desk stood in the corner of the room, but there were no stairs.

"Interesting," murmured Conner. He noticed that the only light in the room was pointed at the wall on his left.

Vincent watched Conner's eyes. "I know what you are thinking," he said calmly. With a heave, he kicked the wall as hard as he could. When the dust settled, a staircase was revealed.

"Ha!" called Conner. "I'll go first."

The group walked up the stairs. Finally, they reached a small hatch.

Conner turned toward them and whispered orders. "Travis, watch the hatch and the staircase. If you need help, just give a yell. Vincent, wait a moment for us to charge. Then, use your rifle to take out the guards. James, stay back and assist Vincent. Jackson, stay back. I don't want you to get hurt…"

"No! I stand by you, brother!" called Jackson.

"All right," Conner shrugged off the fear in his heart. "Jackson and I will charge."

The twins opened the hatch quietly and climbed out. They saw that the guards were moving toward the entrance of the building they were in. An unsuspecting soldier in front of them didn't notice that he was missing a grenade from his belt. Conner passed it down to Travis. "Blow the stairs!"

Travis pulled the pin and threw the grenade. "Get out of there now!" called Jackson.

The men hiding under the hatch got out and put the hatch back into place only seconds before the bang was heard.

The building rocked, throwing the men into each other. Now out in the open, the group was quickly noticed. They dove to a catwalk before responding grenades ripped the top of the building away from them. However, their rifles quickly responded. A fast burst of gunfire annihilated the ten guards sent to the bottom floor. However, Vincent's rifle was hit by a bullet and was sent flying over the rails. He drew his pistol, but his hand was struck by another bullet, sending the pistol flying over the edge as well. He groaned in agony and fell to the ground to nurse his wound. Conner patted him on the head.

"Are you all right?"

Vincent grimaced as he drew the bullet from his hand. "Nothing major. I'll stay behind."

* * * * *

Wilhelm groaned in anger. "How much longer?"

Private Cossack beckoned the six remaining guards to form a protective line in front of von Schreider. "We have seven minutes."

"This is taking too long. I must activate one of the defenses."

He ran to the control room and sat at the desk. He glanced at the three defense buttons. Gates, Catwalks, and Covering were his options. He put his finger down on "Covering".

A large steel wall came up from the ground and surrounded the missile. Smiling, he pressed "Gates". The catwalks that led to the main platform were closed off by large iron gates. Wilhelm reached under the desk, drew a rifle from it, and ran to the main platform.

* * * * *

"Hey!" yelled Conner angrily. "The nerve of that coward! He closed off the catwalks!"

Travis tried to climb over the gate. "Give me a boost!"

Jackson boosted Travis over the gate. Conner jumped to his brother's shoulders and jumped over. He smacked the ground hard and pressed a button on the side of the gate. The gate was immediately destroyed, and Jackson was able to join his comrades.

Wilhelm barked an order to the soldiers. "Move out! Find cover!"

The men took cover behind the missile. James cried out a few words of caution. "Don't shoot the missile, or it'll leak and kill us all!"

Wilhelm snuck behind a pile of cement blocks and watched as the Americans advanced. He growled in anger and watched as two of his soldiers fell to the ground.

He waited silently as one of the men walked past the cement blocks, not noticing him. Taking advantage of the moment, he drew the sword from his belt and went into full view of the rest of the Americans, holding his hostage in front of him.

"Drop your weapons!" he growled angrily.

The men dropped their weapons, and the German soldiers moved forward cautiously.

Wilhelm laughed. "Not so cocky now, are you, *Americans*?" he spat in disgust.

He didn't notice Vincent peering around the corner at him.

He closed his eyes. "Private Cossack, how much time do we have?"

"Four minutes and twenty-four seconds."

Vincent mustered up his courage and ran toward Wilhelm. He was too quick for Wilhelm. He kicked him in the face and freed Conner, who retrieved his rifle and killed four of the remaining guards. Jackson finished off the last two, but then, the group heard a shot, and a cry of pain.

Wilhelm pushed Vincent's corpse away from him and wiped his hands on his pants disdainfully. Conner was in so much shock that he couldn't raise his rifle to shoot Wilhelm as he fled to his control room with Private Cossack.

Conner ground his teeth together as James knelt next to the missile. "We have three and a half minutes."

Chapter 23
Countdown

Wilhelm groped under the desk for a grenade. "This should do what I want," he said, his voice almost giddy as he watched Conner, Jackson, and Travis run to the catwalk. He pulled the pin and threw it onto the catwalk.

Conner threw the others back a split second before it exploded. They gripped the rails for support.

At that moment, Wilhelm let his hand fall upon the last button remaining.

The catwalk rails fell away. Only Travis managed to stay on the catwalk. Conner and Jackson were flung over the edge, barely managing to grip the edge. However, their weapons were flung over the edge. Travis stood, unarmed, as Wilhelm walked toward him, the legendary Boyd sword in his hand.

With nowhere to hide, Travis could only wait for Wilhelm to thrust the blade into his chest. Instead of doing that, Wilhelm pushed him over the edge. He barely got a grip upon it, prolonging his death.

Private Cossack ran across the catwalk to Wilhelm and stopped next to him. "Wilhelm," he said. "Kill them so we can get out of here, sir!"

Conner mustered up his strength and gripped the private's leg. Unprepared for this, the man lost his balance and fell over the edge, barely missing Conner. The scream lasted for almost five seconds, and ended with a sickening crunch.

Wilhelm stepped back to become out of reach of the men. "It's too bad you American's don't learn," he said quietly as he walked over to James and threw him over the edge to join his fellows. "Now, let me end your lives so you miss the destruction of your country.

The sword began its trip down. And then, all of a sudden, a single shot was heard.

Vincent was lying on the ground, his eyes barely open, with his sniper rifle in hand. The men watched in awe as Wilhelm knelt, looking at his bloody chest, and tumbled silently over the edge to join Private Cossack.

Conner hauled himself over the edge and aided his friends to their feet. They ran over to Vincent and knelt at his side.

"Vincent, Vincent!"

He only responded by blinking his eyes.

"Hang in there," called Conner through his tears as James ran to the control room.

"We've got thirty seconds! Self destructing in five, four, three, two, one!"

The missile's rockets powered up and shot it several hundred feet into the air. Then, with a huge boom, it exploded harmlessly.

* * * * *

Commander Dixon said a silent prayer as the helicopter neared the missile. Suddenly, a loud explosion was heard. The pilot laughed into the radio. "General, the missile has been destroyed! I repeat, the missile has been destroyed!"

The helicopter set down on the main platform and the strike team began to disembark.

* * * * *

Conner helped one of the team members ease Vincent into a small cot in the plane. When they were all ready to leave, Conner remembered something.

"Wait a moment for me."

He ran down the spiral staircase and walked to Wilhelm's body. He looked around briefly and saw the sword, stuck point first into the ground. Conner heaved it out of the ground, cleaned it off, and slipped it into its sheath at his side. Then, Conner ran back to the plane. The last team member placed a bomb onto the catwalks. "All right, take off. We're blowing this place away!"

The helicopter took off. Five minutes later, as it steadily flew away from the base, Conner looked back and watched the building explode, never again to harm the United States of America.

Chapter 24
Press Release

Eight days later, at the military base
Richmond, Virginia
10:00 a.m.

"Thank you, ladies and gentlemen!" called General Starr. "Thank you!"

He was standing at a podium, giving a speech to the press. "Several weeks ago," he began, "two young recruits named Conner and Jackson Boyd volunteered to journey to some of the coastal cities to free them from the Germans."

"Unfortunately, their mission failed, and they were shot down over Fragul. They were the only ones to survive the crash. However, they managed to uncover one of Germany's main bases there, and radioed us to destroy it. They managed to escape to Aurich in a plane occupied by several Germans, and they traveled to Rhaude by plane. They uncovered another base there, and they met an assassin named Vincent Stenvich, a young soldier named Travis McCarthy, and a British man named James Farion who possessed important information about a weapon that the Germans were planning to use; a virus called Mandible."

A ripple moved through the crowd.

"The Germans planned to launch it at the United States. However, thanks to those four, the missile was destroyed. Now, I would like to honor the men who made our country safe."

He cleared his throat.

"Conner and Jackson Boyd!"

The crowd clapped as the two came onto the stage. General Starr shook their hands and put medals around their necks. "This man endured torture and German prison to protect our country's secrets and destroy the virus that was intended to kill us all; James Farion!"

James walked onto the stage, with his little boy, Rodger, in his arms. General Starr kissed the baby's forehead and put the medal around his neck.

"This man was my replacement after the mutiny against me until I recovered. Private David McCarthy and his brother, Private Travis McCarthy!"

The two walked on stage and accepted their medals gratefully.

"Finally, the brave assassin who risked his life for the men he was assigned to protect and saved that last bullet. Introducing the honorable Vincent Stenvich!"

The assassin walked onto the stage, bearing a bandaged hand and a heavily cushioned chest. Smiling, he took the medal and stood with his comrades.

"There you have it," said General Starr. "Give it up for these loyal men!"

The crowd roared appreciatively.

"Though this man died in battle, we honor him today. His name was Steven Johnson."

There was silence for a moment.

"Thank you for coming. You are dismissed."

The buzz of conversation began as everyone began to talk about the speech.

Conner and Jackson were silent for a moment. Then, they looked at each other.

"Conner," asked Jackson, "don't you want to go back home and just live a normal life?"

"Yeah," agreed Conner.

General Starr walked up to them. "I completely understand if you would like to leave the military. The war is over now."

Conner drew the sword from its sheath and looked it over pensively. "Yes, General. Just call us when you need us."

The men walked away, leaving their past behind.

The legend will continue.

About the Author

Matthew Reade is an eleven-year old author who lives in Northern California with his family. He is an avid reader; he enjoys reading fantasy, science fiction, and historical fiction novels. His hobbies include reading, writing, playing videogames, and golfing. He has already written two books, *John: Son of a Commander* and *Clone 71: The Brotherhood*, and doesn't plan on stopping his writing career anytime soon.

 www.ingramcontent.com/pod-product-compliance
Ingram Content Group UK Ltd.
Pitfield, Milton Keynes, MK11 3LW, UK
UKHW051254180426
11947UKWH00020B/1713